Motherfucker

MJ Marstens

Contents

Dedication

To all the amazing and real nuns and priests in my life who made a difference. Sister Michael, I'm thirty-two and I still remember my freshman year of high school like it was yesterday and whenever I think of those times, I see your face. I also see khaki pants and Mr. Elsner's hairy chest, but I see your sweet goodness.

Thank you for letting me be me. You knew that I was a pagan heathen deep inside and you encouraged me to embrace that. You also encouraged me to pet my cat, not my date. Those words still stick with me. In fact, I used them in my *Afflicted Zodiac* series.

Also, I can't look at a tomato without seeing it sing in my head thanks to the countless hours that we watched Veggie Tales in your religion class. Now I know that God is bigger than the boogeyman. As an adult, it just sounds like God's dick is bigger than the boogeyman's, but my head's totally not in the gutter or anything.

Also, this is for Sister Agnes. You sweet, poor lady. Why the hell did you think that your calling was high school math? Teaching is already a thankless job, but calculus for the reluctant? Seriously, you were a nice lady, but I feel like God was punishing you hardcore for some shit.

I hope that you escaped and are now nunning it up on some tropical island surrounded by hot, sweaty priests. Nevermind, that's just my personal fantasy, but I truly hope that you are doing well. Maybe retired? Not teaching asshole high schoolers. . .

Speaking of asshole high schoolers, Deacon Sialer, remember when the fucksticks in your religion class would all bang on their desks together to trigger your PTSD from Vietnam? Just thinking about it still pisses me off. What a bunch of douche canoes. And for the record: I totally believe that you saw Sasquatch.

And lastly, thank you to Father Andres. Remember in your junior year religion class that paper we had to write about another religion? I chose Wicca and you told me that wasn't a real religion, but a Satanic Cult, but I wrote my paper on it anyway. . . And you were pissed, my family was pissed, and I'm still obviously pissed, haha.

Well, thanks. And I mean that. Thank you for shoving my stubborn ass headlong into the very thing that makes me happy. Now, I'm not Wiccan, more a free-spirited hippy/pagan heathen who is too lazy to really adhere

VIII

or abide by any religious dogma, but I was so turned off by your closed-mindedness, by your refusal to better understand another's viewpoint (which, I might point out, was the whole point of the paper), that I promised that I would never do that.

Your intolerance actually made me more tolerant.

And, I said it sixteen years ago and I will say it today: Wicca has nothing to do with Satan.

But this book?

Totally the work of the Devil.

A Long-winded Foreword

When I was eight, my parents transferred me to a Catholic school. The previous year, when I had my First Communion and stole a bracelet (which my Grandma refused to buy to match my dress) from the store, that should have been my parents' first clue that Catholicism and MJ weren't jiving.*

Actually, their first clue should have been my obsession with the occult, my ridiculously large rock collection, and penchant for dressing up like a witch even when it wasn't Halloween, but I digress.

Catholic school wasn't bad, but there were strict rules of conformity that I simply didn't fit into. At the time, I didn't really know any better. I was a consummate people-pleaser, so as I grew older, I tried to fit myself into this religious mold, but I never could get comfortable.

Maybe it was the horrible uniforms with the school colors (Go ahead and envision a bulky brown jumper with a golden plaid design), or maybe it was the fact that our mascot was The Trojan. . . that's right: we looked like a school of shitty condoms.

But more than likely, it was my encounters with people within the church itself that turned me away. Specifically, in third grade, when we were helping the second graders prepare for their First Communion. The priest had us line up to be 'pretend priests' and offer 'The Body of Christ' to the second graders to practice receiving it for the first time.

Looking back, I realize that I was the only girl in the line.

When it got to be my turn, I used my deepest pretend-priest voice and said, "Body of Christ", but the priest cut me off and succinctly told me that women couldn't be priests. Even to pretend, *but* I could be a bride of Christ.

You know when someone tries to church up something you know is second-rate?

Yeah, that's exactly how I felt then and now.

At nine years old, I felt like a second-class citizen in my faith.

It only got worse.

I was always asking the 'wrong' questions: If God's love is *unconditional,* then how is everyone not in Heaven? Where the fuck was Jesus between the ages of ten and thirty-three? Why *can't* I own and operate a midget brothel?!

It wasn't until I got older and pulled away from my religious family that I realized that I'm not a religious person at all.

I'm spiritual as fuck, but religious?

Nope.

I adhere that life just wants you to be a good person.

A kind person.

A, how you say, not a petty cuntcushion.

But make no mistake that I don't respect other faiths and the people that serve within them.

I sincerely have the utmost respect for the individuals that genuinely dedicate their lives to becoming a better person and bettering the world around them.

Having said that, I must confess that I have a thing for hot priests.

Of all my taboos, nothing gets my non-existent panties in a twist like the thought of some fatherly fucking. I dream of them dousing me with their holy water. . .

TMI?

My bad.

Well, I'll just let you get along with your reading. Please know that it's meant to be a satirical piece that pokes fun at religion, but isn't meant to be truly offensive. Unless you consider priest porn and nun nooky sacrilegious. . . in which case, how did you get your hands on my book?

That cover should have said it all.

To everyone else: *enjoy.*

*So, my Grandma marched my thieving ass right back up to the store and made me confess to the woman working what I had done, and the lady smiled and said it was all right. My Grandma was so pissed at the woman for telling me that it was ok to steal (especially whilst shopping for First Communion goods), that she returned everything on the spot and I got nothing that day. Fucking bully for her, because that shit ain't cool- stealing and telling a kid that it's ok to do so. My Grandma took a stand and said, 'Not today, Satan!'.

Chapter 1

The Pissy Last Straw

I was fucked.

And I didn't mean in the good way, with 'my ass in the air and my face to the headboard getting railed' fucked.

I didn't even mean the 'I messed up big time and made a huge mistake' fucked.

I meant 'I'm going to die, literally' fucked.

The worst kind of fucked to be, and all because I was an idiot.

At thirty-three, I knew better than to trust someone.

Three decades of living on the streets taught you that lesson very quickly. The only person I could trust was myself. So why the fuck did I trust the document forger my MC club used?

Clearly, because *I* was an idiot.

A *delusional* idiot, at that, because I tried to bribe the forger. Obviously, he was way smarter than me. Whatever funds I had, the club had- only ten times more. It really was a no-brainer that the forger went to Walker, the club's president and my 'owner'.

And that's how Walker found out I had opened an account and was slowly siphoning funds into it. Now, I was a dead woman. So much for planning for a better future, which is what I had been doing when I made that new account. Usually, I would never have been so rash, but I finally threw in the towel that fateful night three weeks ago.

It was a normal evening at the local bar the club owned. I was working, but not behind the counter or on the stage. No, I was Walker's special pet. His personal whore. He derived untold pleasure from making this known. Where he paid the other girls for their services, whether they were legal or not, I never saw a dime.

Not a single one in all the years I'd been at Walker's side.

He had nabbed me at fourteen; so, that's nineteen long years being his complimentary bitch.

Usually, Walker liked to keep me to himself, but occasionally, when another club president would come in for trades or negotiations, he would 'lease' me out for the night. A special 'thank you' for doing business with him.

These interactions always stung.

Don't mistake me; I had no visions of grandeur where Walker was concerned. I didn't love him and he sure as shit didn't love me, but I thought we had *something*. A friendship, a bond, *anything* to indicate I was more than just a hole for him. Of course, there's my delusional ass trying to make a shit situation better.

I *was* just a hole.

A free one.

A complacent one.

So, when Walker handed me over to the president of the Los Matadores, I didn't bat an eyelash. It was just my fervent hope that the tattooed bastard didn't like it violent. Rough I liked, violent- no thanks. I enjoy keeping my blood inside me and walking without wheezing from a cracked rib.

The burly Mexican MC president barely spoke English, but he knew enough to get what he wanted. In a private room down the hall from the bustling bar area, he commanded me to my knees. In stilted English, he ordered me to shut my eyes and open my mouth- tongue out.

7

I was kind of surprised.

This guy had *violent* written all over him, but I guess a standard money shot to my face was going to be good enough. I shrugged it off and did as I was told. With any luck, he would get off and be done for the evening. Maybe I could go back to the complex early tonight.

When nothing happened after I heard the guy unzip himself, I stealthy cracked an eye open.

Thank fuck I did.

In just the nick of time, I saw his intention.

The bastard was going to *piss* on me!

At the last second, I snapped my mouth shut and turned my face, my right cheek catching the brunt of his stream. His grunt of disapproval didn't cover his groan of pleasure as he doused me. The sound echoed off the walls of the room; my gagging soon following. I knew that I was likely going to get a backhand to the face for not following instructions, but I would have vomited all over the sick fuck's feet if he had peed in my mouth.

Mr. Goldenshower finally finished, and as predicted, landed a hard smack across my face. The blow sent me over, and I landed in a heap in the puddle of piss around my body. A few drops of the golden nastiness managed to splash into my mouth when I cried out at the impact.

Mother.

Fucker.

The nasty bastard let out a satisfied chuckle and kicked me swiftly in the side with his steel-toed boot, but thankfully, he left me alone with my shredded dignity.

Minutes later, Walker sauntered in.

"That's fucking disgusting. Go home and get yourself cleaned up. The sight of you covered in piss makes my skin crawl."

The man had cut another human's intestines from their gut, but *I* made his skin crawl?

The sheer irony of it wasn't lost on me as Walker stomped out, slamming the door.

It was then I decided that I was done.

I went back to the complex and scrubbed my body until my skin was raw, then I sat and planned. Ideas had come and gone in the past, but I never really thought to make my dreams of 'escape' a reality. More like it was just wishful thinking, something to pass the time. I knew that I wasn't destined for more.

9

I was the daughter of a crack whore, my father-unknown.

The state took me from my mother when I was barely half a year old. It's actually scary to think that she'd had me for that long. From that point on, I was in and out of foster care. At thirteen, I ran away, not able to cope with the abuse. Abuse, which stemmed from my appearance.

Everyone used to tell me how lucky I was to be beautiful.

I was a *real looker*, they said.

Pft, all my looks ever did for me was get me molested.

I would take being 'ugly' any day of the week.

Ugly girls worked behind the scenes.

Ugly girls were left alone.

Ugly girls survived.

Pretty girls were worked; their scars growing every day on the inside. Eventually, either the external abuse or the internal damage did them in. Usually, it was the internal damage. The women couldn't take it anymore. They would turn to drugs, pill-popping, and when it got bad enough, if those things didn't kill them, they would do it themselves.

I've seen so many good girls get hooked on drugs it's not even funny.

It's the only thing I've never done.

My promise to myself.

So far, I've managed, but barely.

Walker's tried to get me hooked many times.

He thought it would make me more pliable.

What a joke.

I was already pliable.

When he found me running on the streets a year after being on my own, I was broken down and afraid. At the time, his father was the MC's president and Walker was vice-president. Young and full of swagger, I loved the confidence that Walker had then. He was badass and he knew it.

For once, my looks did me a favor. Walker was driving through my neighborhood and just happened to see me. He twisted his bike around onto the sidewalk and stopped in front of me. He took off his sunglasses, his light eyes piercing into mine.

"Wanna get away from here?" he offered.

His handsome face made my head swim; his offer damn near made me pass out.

"If you come with me, you work for me, but I'll protect you. No one will lay a finger on you."

Those were the magic words that I needed to hear.

I needed a champion and Walker became mine that day.

I didn't question his price.

I knew what 'working' for him meant, but I was glad to give myself freely to someone by *my* choice. For a few years, my life actually improved. And maybe once upon a time, I idolized Walker. Maybe even crushed on him hard.

I wouldn't call it love.

I don't think someone like me is capable of loving, but I will admit to being infatuated.

Until his dad died and Walker became president of The Outcasts of Hell.

Then his promise that no one would ever lay a finger on me became conditional.

No one would ever lay a finger on me without *his permission.*

And just like that, my freedom was gone.

Looking back, I wondered how I could have foolishly ever thought I had any to begin with.

Chapter 2

Plan B Fuck-up

Walker didn't return to the complex that night. It was as if fate itself wanted me to succeed. After I washed that shitbag's piss off me, I dried off and headed to the room that I shared with Walker. Being his pet certainly had its privileges, but really it was for his convenience. Like in case he wanted a quick fuck when he woke up or needed something done 'with a woman's touch', as he called it.

Basically, any type of bitch work.

Cooking, cleaning, sucking cock.

I was a glorified housekeeping slut.

I was also the only woman at the complex.

All the other members had rooms but usually went to their houses to be with their families.

I wasn't Walker's 'old lady', but I was accorded some of that respect, at least. Generally, I was left alone. Partly, because everyone feared Walker's wrath, and partly because they thought I was cursed goods.

Some nonsense about me being the granddaughter of The Don, the leader of the Sicilian Mafia here in Southern California.

The Outcasts of Hell feared The Don would come looking for me and would retaliate against the MC.

That pipe dream of mine died years ago.

Ain't nobody looking for me.

Not then.

Not now.

I was given access to all of the complex but I mostly stayed in Walker's room. It was the only place without cameras. And it had his personal computer. I spent a long time convincing Walker I was stupid. It actually didn't take much, looking back, but I wanted him to really think that I was mentally incompetent.

I cracked a smile at the thought.

I must have been convincing enough because a few of the older club members always spoke very slowly to me. It took everything inside me not to bust up.

Or cry when I walked away and they talked about my only worth being my fine ass and big titties.

Fuck them.

I knew my worth.

I spent hours teaching myself how to use Walker's computer.

I learned his passwords, figured out how to hack shit, and eventually came across his bank accounts.

His *overseas* bank accounts.

Being an MC president is some good business.

You run some legal shit as a front and fucking make bank on the illegal crap.

Guns, drugs, women, you name it, and Walker had a hand in all of it.

And boy, did it line his pockets.

In fact, his pockets were so fucking deep, he wouldn't even notice fifty-thousand dollars missing.

I kind of wanted to crap myself at the number, but that's pocket change to Walker.

Yet, that pocket change was my ticket out of there.

My freedom.

It had taken me thirty-three years to grow a set of balls, but I finally did it.

I moved some money around and created a new off-shore account under a false name.

All I needed was some documentation.

A new identification.

A quick visit to the club's forger would solve that, as long as I convinced him I was there on Walker's behalf.

I didn't.

The slick bastard saw right through me.

So I moved onto Plan B, which I made up right then on the spot: *bribery.*

I thought it had worked until I left. I took the long way home to the complex, making plans. Escape plans. Future plans. So many plans. I was distracted and excited, but the sound of a bike pulled me from my thoughts. Bikes always got my attention.

When I looked behind me, I saw a sleek-looking number zipping up the road, but it wasn't the bike that caught my attention.

It was the rider.

He was wearing an Outcasts of Hell jacket.

And was pulling a gun from it.

I might pretend to be stupid, but I'm not.

I knew who those bullets were meant for.

Moving quickly, I ducked and rolled into the closest open window-well of a brick apartment as the driver zoomed by, shooting slug after slug in my general direction. He whipped a shitty at the stop sign some seventy-five yards up the road and I scrambled to gather my wits.

Kicking in the broken window, and praying I didn't get shot for breaking and entering into someone's place, I slipped inside. Maybe if I escaped out the back, I could run and get away.

Maybe.

I made my way through the basement apartment not encountering anyone, luckily, and unlocked the door. Before I stepped through, the sound of more gunfire arrested my attention. Slowly, cautiously, I inched back to the window.

People from the apartment had come out.

Turf wars were a very serious thing here in San Bernardino.

About six or seven guys were chasing after the club member, shooting.

I crawled back out the window and ran in the direction I had originally come from. I ran and ran, only stopping to slip off my high heels. The overcast sky finally unleashed its torrent, helping to mask me even more.

I ran for miles.

An overpass came into view and I jogged under it to catch my breath. Standing there was a nun in a sopping wet habit. She beckoned me forward.

"Come on and get out of this rain," she called over the roaring wind.

I stepped under the concrete bridge and the woman pulled me to her side.

I blinked in apprehension.

I didn't really like people touching me, especially strangers, but I realized she was just trying to warm me up.

"Child, this is a terrible outfit to wear in this weather," she chides in a motherly tone.

A stressed giggle escaped me.

It was a terrible outfit to wear *whenever*.

I looked like a "classy hooky".

Heels, stockings with the seam up the back, a short leather skirt that looked painted on, and a simple long-sleeve white shirt. The thick material of the top made it so the fabric wasn't see-through in the rain, but the wetness practically plastered the shirt to me and outlined my lacy bra underneath.

I had wanted to seem "professional" in front of the forger so that he would take me seriously.

Stupid, stupid, stupid.

The nun and I stood huddled together in silence as the storm raged on around us. I rested my cheek against her shoulder and for the first time in forever, I felt safe.

Even cared for, a little.

"I'm Raelynn," I mumbled.

"Sister Evangeline," she returned.

"*Evangeline*," I tested. "What a pretty name."

"It means 'angel of good news'; it's where the word 'evangelist' comes from, or one who spreads the gospel."

I didn't know what my name meant.

I hadn't even thought of it until now.

Did it mean 'daughter of a crack whore'?

I was drawn from my musings when the familiar hum of a bike engine revving sounded over the thunder.

The club member was back!

Childishly, I cowered behind the nun, trying to hide my form behind her voluminous black skirts. Maybe the guy wouldn't see me. The sweet woman backed me against the wall, caging me in behind her, protecting me.

The bike zipped by without incident.

It was so fast that I couldn't make out who it was in the dark of the storm, but it must have been an Outcast of Hell because two speeding cars came chasing after it, guns still firing. True to their motto of 'Fear Nothing', the club member whipped around and came racing back at the two black cars.

More shooting ensued and someone's scream cut through the air.

I felt a chill crawl down my spine at the sound.

It was *me* screaming.

Then it was silent once more and only my harsh breathing could be heard.

The nun was slumped against me and I was afraid she must have passed out. I pushed my way from out behind her and lightly tapped her cheek, trying to awaken her.

I pulled at her collar, thinking the damn thing was too tight, but in the faint light of the fading evening, I saw the truth.

Her neck was stained red and torn open from where a bullet had pierced it.

Chapter 3

The Blasphemous Lie

"Evangeline!" I yelled and I watched her eyelids weakly flutter.

"Raelynn," she whispered. "Get some. . . where safe."

Her breathing became labored as she tried to speak, her life force spilling out faster and faster with each passing second.

I'd seen enough death to know that this kind woman wouldn't make it.

"No," I sobbed, not wanting to let her go.

She had protected me and I had been a coward.

"Go," she urged. "You can find san. . . sanctuary at. . . The Immaculate Heart of Mary. They are waiting for me to arrive."

It was hard to understand her as her voice became fainter and fainter.

"Take my cross and go with Gabriel. God bless you, sweet child."

And then she was gone.

I sat there, sobbing uncontrollably before I pulled myself together.

She was right.

I wasn't safe here.

With shaking hands, I gently took off the golden crucifix around her neck before I internalized her other words.

Gabrielle?

Who was she?

I looked around, thinking maybe there was another nun under the bridge that I had missed, but I didn't see anyone. Shrugging it off, I got up to walk away. On impulse, I turned back to give the woman one last hug and then I grabbed her suitcase. Giving it to someone seemed like the least I could do, instead of leaving it to be pilfered by the next person who passed it.

At the edge of the bridge, I hesitated.

The rain had yet to abate and made an effective curtain to hide behind for a few more minutes. I hastily opened the suitcase, looking for money. My guts twisted in agony. Stealing was wrong, but stealing from a nun? That shit got you personally escorted to Hell by God himself.

But desperate times call for desperate measures.

I rifled through the woman's belongings, yet all I found were a couple of habits, one black and one white, a rosary, and a prayer book. Slamming the thing shut, I couldn't tell if I was relieved or disappointed. I needed the money, but now I wasn't stealing from one of God's Chosen Ladies.

Suddenly, an idea burst into my head.

I quickly unlatched the suitcase once more and pulled out the black habit.

It would make the perfect disguise until I could get somewhere to tell someone what happened.

I yanked it over my head and smoothed on the headdress, hoping I had everything right.

I was basing it off a dead nun.

I grimaced.

I mean, I was already going to hell, but this shit right here?

It sealed the deal.

I popped my attempt at professionalism into the suitcase and snapped it shut. Then, I ran into the rain. I had no idea where I was going, but I needed to get out of Del Rosa, the neighborhood that I was in. The Outcasts of Hell's complex was on the outskirts, backed by the desert- the perfect place to dispose of bodies.

But the neighborhood itself was bad news.

Full of gangs and crime.

I made it a few more blocks and finally crossed Highway 210. This was the city's demarcation between good and evil. Once I crossed the highway, a terrifying feat in itself, it was as if the backdrop to civilization had returned. Working street lights, windows without bars, people walking around with umbrellas.

A taxi cab went splashing by me and suddenly slammed on its brakes. The red lights damn near blinded me as it backed up until the passenger door was next to me.

The window rolled down and the cabby called from inside, "Heya Sister! Can I take you somewhere? This weather is a nightmare."

I hesitated, noticing the cross dangling from his rearview mirror.

Of course, this didn't mean he was a nice guy.

Plenty of people hid behind this hallowed symbol, rotten to their very cores, their holier-than-thou exterior hiding the horrors that lay inside, but I had no idea where I was going. I was cold, lost, and scared.

I hadn't been this frightened since the night I decided to run away.

So, questioning my judgment for a second time that day, I jumped into the backseat of the cab, keeping my head down. Although the rain had probably already washed all my makeup off, I was sure nuns didn't look like me.

"Where to, Sister?"

"Ah. . . The Immaculate Heart of Mary. . . but I-I-I don't have any money-"

"Don't you worry about that, Sister!" the man cut me off. "I was heading home for the night anyway and I drive right past the convent. It's a bit of a distance from here, though. Another twenty minutes or so."

I could hear the question in his voice, but I kept my head bowed.

"Thank you," I whispered in heartfelt appreciation.

I watched the world zip by me, wondering how I was going to break the news to the other nuns about their friend. When the taxi slowed down in front of a gorgeous stone building, I still didn't have an answer.

"Here you are, Sister," the cabbie announced.

He got out of the cab and even opened the door for me.

I took his proffered hand and slid out of the backseat. Giving him a small squeeze, I expressed my genuine gratitude. The cab driver smiled and wished me a good-night before driving away. I walked up the path to the gate and buzzed the intercom.

"The Immaculate Heart of Mary, how can I help you?" a voice called out.

"I'm. . ." I trailed off, uncertain of what to say. "Sister Evangeline sen-"

"Oh, thank heavens, Sister! Come right in! We've been expecting you *for hours*."

The gates swung open and I briskly went in, thankful to be out of the rain. I would explain the mix-up when I got inside. Surely, they would understand, wouldn't they?

Understanding and forgiveness were a nun's bread and butter, right? I wasn't really sure though. Those few years I spent with a church-going family were not memories that I ever wished to revisit.

A nun met me at the door.

"Hi! I'm Sister Agatha; welcome. I'm sorry to meet on such sad circumstances, but Mother Catherine is still awake and wants to see you."

I nodded, confused.

Sad circumstances?

Did they already know about Sister Evangeline?

Sister Agatha led me through a main area and then up some stairs and down a long hall. Knocking softly on a large door, she opened it to reveal a sparsely furnished room. In fact, all that there was inside it was a bed, a dresser, and a prayer corner with a place to kneel, but the walls were richly decorated in different religious paintings and one window sported a beautiful stained glass piece depicting the crucifixion of Jesus.

At least, I thought that's what it was, but my attention was drawn to the figures inside the room. On the bed, snuggled under several layers of blankets, was a very sickly-looking nun, and next to the bed, there was a positively ancient-looking priest.

"Sister Evangeline!" the voice rasped from the bed. "Thank you, Sister Agatha."

"You're so very welcome, Mother. I am. . . just going to go pray some more," Sister Agatha announced tearfully, shutting the door quietly behind her.

The elderly priest lumbered to his feet.

"Welcome, Sister. I'm Father McMann. I'm retired, but live in the rectory next to the convent. I administer the sacraments and do a daily mass here for the sisters and the community. Nice to meet you," he greeted, holding out a hand for me to shake.

Suddenly, it dawned on me:

No one knew Sister Evangeline.

She was on her way to the convent but never made it.

No one here had a clue about what had happened and I knew that the kind sister's body was long gone.

In Del Rosa, evidence was never left to be found.

Either someone from the MC or whoever else was shooting had come along to dispose of the corpse.

Internally, I battled myself, but my need for survival won.

I had nowhere else to go, even the police were infiltrated with the MC's spies.

I knew it was wrong.

The wrongest of the wrong, but again, what was one more mark against my already damned soul?

I shook the priest's hand.

"I'm Sister Evangeline. It's nice to finally meet you, Father."

Chapter 4

Smooth Sinner

That lie sealed my fate and paved the way for where I am now:

Sitting in the abbess' office, head of The Immaculate Heart of Mary.

Can you believe this shit?

It turns out, Mother Catherine was *dying* and Sister Evangeline was her replacement.

I arrived that night just in time to watch Father McMann administer the final rites for the woman, for her to give me her blessing, and then she passed rather peacefully.

The whole convent grieved their loss, but rebounded quickly, embracing me as their new Mother.

Now, a week later, I sit behind Mother Catherine's desk, at a complete loss of what the fuck to do.

I barely know how to be a human being, let alone one that is supposed to be a decent, God-fearing nun.

A knock sounds at the door and I call the person in.

It's Sister Mary-Francis.

"Good morning, Mother," she greets me, and I try my damndest, I mean darndest, not to flinch.

"Morning, Sister. What can I do for you?"

"Father McMann mentioned you might need some help getting settled."

Well, that was a fucking understatement.

"Yes, I do. Things here are, ah, very different. In fact, the more I think about it, you might be more suited for this position. I'm thinking of just demoting myself and you can step up."

Sister Mary-Francis looks at me in horror, then her face clears, and she tips her head back in laughter.

"Oh, Mother! What a wicked sense of humor you have. Shame!" she teases to my astonishment. "I'll have to warn the other sisters."

I let out a nervous chuckle.

"Ahahaha, you caught me. I'm a. . . funny one. Anyway, where should we start?"

"Sister Agnes keeps the books, so all the accounting should be up to snuff. I think there are some grants for you to review and maybe some letters from the diocese that Mother Catherine did not get to in her last days."

She makes the sign of the cross at the mention of the late abbess.

I sloppily copy her.

"Great. I mean, 'great' about the other stuff, not Mother Catherine dying."

Wow.

I'm a smooth sinner.

Not.

"What do you do, Sister Mary-Francis?"

"I'm the community outreach. It's the closest I can get to being a therapist," she says a little sadly.

"Can nuns not be therapists?" I ask dumbly before remembering *a Mother* should know things like this. "I mean, uh-"

"I like you, Mother Evangeline. You're really blunt; you don't need to explain yourself. I petitioned the diocese a few years back to continue my schooling so that I could get my degree, but my request was denied."

I twitch, feeling like she slapped me.

I hate when people are told they can't do something.

"Did they say why?" I ask her, wondering what the hell kind of cult I'd gotten myself involved in.

I'm fucked if they have Kool-Aid.

There ain't no way I can say no to that shit.

Black cherry is my jam.

"Yes, they said that they didn't have the funds. I would need a master's degree. I could take online classes, but I know the diocese has a strict budget for these kinds of things. There's definitely a need, but. . ."

"Maybe you should ask again," I suggest and she shakes her head.

I hate the defeated look on her face.

All the women at the convent have been so nice to me so far.

There are seven of them in total.

Sister Agatha, Sister Agnes, Sister Mary-Francis, Sister María Concepción, Sister Bernadette, Sister Rachel, and Sister Patricia.

Sister Patricia and Sister María Concepción are the Spanish-speaking liaisons to the community. As mendicants, the sisters serve the surrounding neighborhoods, spreading God's word and helping those in need, while living in poverty. Sister Rachel cooks; Sister Bernadette teaches, and Sister Agatha is the center's 'receptionist'.

"What if I asked?" I offered, not even having the first clue of how to go about it.

Sister Mart-Francis' face lights up.

"You wouldn't mind?"

"No, I have a connection in the diocese," I bluff.

She nods her head sagely.

"That explains why someone so young got the position."

I grimace.

Oh, fuck.

I knew it wouldn't take them long to question my looks. . .

"Can I just say you don't look thirty-eight," she compliments

"That's because I'm thirty-three," I correct, then blush.

Motherfucker.

Shut up mouth!

"My three must have looked like an eight," I lie some more, hoping she didn't see "my" birthdate.

It probably wouldn't be wise to lie to her and say that I'm poor at math if I'm the head overseer of the accounts.

"Oh, well, you don't look thirty-three either!" she exclaims and I nod.

"Yeah, everyone thinks I'm way younger."

I look like a freaking teenager.

"Is this going to be a problem?" I wonder out loud.

"Oh no, our convent lowered the age a sister could become a Mother to thirty. As long as you have ten years in first."

"Oh yeah, I took my vows at eighteen."

40

"That's beautiful. I didn't take mine until my mid-twenties. I wasn't sure what I wanted to do with my life, but God called me here. I'm thankful for every day that I get to spend it with you and my sisters."

I smile at her sincerity.

Damned if I don't get Sister Mary-Francis into graduate school, now.

"When do classes start?" I ask her.

"I actually have already been accepted into the program, so if I had the money, I could start classes next week! But I know that's a little inconvenient and unfair to expect that with such short notice. If the diocese gives you the go-ahead, I can schedule to start classes in the next eight weeks, which is how long the school's semesters run."

"How much do you need to start up?"

"I need $5,000 down, but there's a scholarship program for students attending. I truly think I could get it, but only those who have completed two eight-week courses can apply. If I'm awarded it, the rest of my schooling would be free!"

Her excitement is palpable.

"Ok, well, let me make some calls. . ."

She squeals in excitement and I can't contain my laugh.

After she leaves, I look over the accounts.

I cringe, taking in the meager amounts.

Walker makes more taking a piss, but it seems the majority of the money comes in from donations.

Obviously, I don't have any fucking connections, but I refuse to let Sister Mary-Francis down. Maybe if we did a community potluck or something, I could raise the money for her.

I meet the sisters downstairs and we go over to the adjacent church for mass.

I mumble the prayers under my breath and go through the motions.

It's been over twenty years since I've been to a mass, but everything is slowly coming back. I hate to acknowledge that time, but I'm slightly grateful for it now. It's the only thing saving my ass from looking like a total fraud.

That, and the internet.

Thank Jesus, his ghostly friend, and the apostles for the internet.

Afterward, I put my plan into motion.

"What does everyone think about having a community potluck to raise money?" I ask everyone as we walk back to the convent.

"Raise money? For what?" Sister Patricia asks in confusion.

"For the poor," I answer smoothly.

"Oh, how wonderful!" Sister Bernadette exclaims. "But everyone that attends the church is poor."

"That's why I'll make flyers and go into town to get newcomers," I state.

"Ooo, you're very progressive, aren't you?" Sister Agnes observes.

"Hell yeah, I am. I'm more Progressive than that insurance bitc- lady."

All the sisters gasp in scandalization and make the sign of the cross.

Whoops.

Chapter 5

Spreading the Legs of God

The potluck was a huge success. I marketed the shit out of it in downtown San Bernardino, promising everything from surf and turf to the rarest and most decadent desserts. A donation was all that was required to enter.

Of course, it wasn't my fault that none of the shit I said would be there wasn't.

It was a potluck.

I couldn't make the participants bring steak and lobster, now could I?

Some folks grumbled, but I already had their money, so I didn't give a fuck.

A total of $3,412 was raised.

That's a lot of money donated.

Or maybe pick-pocketed.

Semantics.

Sister Mary-Francis needed money.

But where was I going to come up with the extra $1,588?

I'm now sitting at a little café close to downtown, thinking and taking a break from *mothering*.

Fake nunning is hard work.

Behind me, two women chat about a wealthy friend and her son's addiction to 'buying women of the night'.

Bingo.

"I'm sorry, ladies. I couldn't help but overhear about your friend. Is there anything I can do?" I offer solicitously, interjecting myself into their conversation.

The one woman looks at me pensively, but the other has a snooty look on her face. Time to nip this shit in the bud.

"Unless you had no intention of helping and you both were just *gossiping?*"

I raise my voice to catch other customers' attention.

Both women immediately shake their heads and look around in horror.

"N-n-no, of course not, sister," the snooty one stutters.

"It's Mother," I correct generously.

Fuck, I am loving this.

"Sorry. Mother. It's our friend. Well, her son."

"So, I heard. Maybe if I spoke with the woman. You could send her to my convent, perhaps."

"No, Lindsay won't leave the house," the other woman responds.

"Well, maybe she could visit her?" the other woman tells her.

"Hmm, I don't generally make house calls, but maybe I could make an exception," I bluff.

"Really? Thank you. Here, let me write down her address."

I try to school my face.

This woman is just going to give me her friend's address because I look like a nun?

Honestly, I shouldn't be surprised.

More shit has been comped to me this week than in my entire life.

They give me her address and I hop on my bike.

Not the kind I'm used to.

This one requires manual pedaling.

It takes about fifteen minutes, but I eventually make my way to a rich-ass neighborhood. Holy shit, these people are rolling in the dough. Walker had money, but you didn't really *see it* like this. I walk up to the giant house with the matching address the woman gave me and I ring the doorbell.

I might not have been able to fool the forger, but normal folks?

I can con the fuck out of them.

Normal folks are naturally trusting.

Add a nun's habit and there's no way I could be a liar.

A very glamorous woman answers the door.

"Lindsay?" I ask.

"Yes, can I help you?"

"I'm just a friend coming by to say that if you need anyone to talk to about your son, I'm here for you."

Apparently, those are the magic words she needs to hear. She invites me in and just unloads her worries on me about how her nineteen-year-old son is dropping *hundreds of thousands* of dollars on hookers.

"Perhaps if Father McMann spoke with him. . ." I ponder.

"Oh, do you think he could help?" Lindsay wonders.

"He has a special degree in intervention counseling," I prevaricate. "I can have him stop by tomorrow night, if that works."

Lindsay's eyes fill with tears.

"Yes, that sounds perfect. Philip and I have a dinner thing in L.A. and it would ease my mind to know that someone is with Philip Jr."

"How does 9pm sound?"

"I'll make sure he's here."

"Perfect," I purr.

I get up to leave and she walks me to the door.

"Thank you again, so much, Mother," she gushes.

"It's nothing. Try not to worry too much. Sometimes kids are going to make you proud and other times, they're going to make you go 'what the fuck', ya know? Alright, go with God and all that crap." I reassure her, waving my hand in the air like I saw the priest do.

Then I depart without a backward glance.

The next night, I excuse myself, telling the sisters that I'm needed for a prayer circle.

They all exclaim how exciting this sounds and to please invite them next time. I promise and leave, wondering how I can organize an actual prayer circle.

When I get halfway across town, I duck into an alley and change into my 'classy hooker' clothes that I stashed in a satchel. Except, I leave out the bra and underwear.

Super classy.

Hopefully, the cloak of night will hide my less than appropriate clothing.

I stuff my habit into my bag and pedal over to Lindsay's house with minutes to spare. I fold my leather skirt under, making it even shorter, and then I ring the doorbell. A young guy opens the door.

"Philip?" I ask.

"Uh, yeah," he answers, his eyes glazing over when he takes in my outfit.

I can honestly say that I've never charged someone for sex.

Walker just took it, the thankless prick.

There's something empowering about doing this.

It's *my* body, *my* choice.

Philip is cute, albeit way too young. I'm nearly *fifteen* years older, but I need *fifteen* hundred dollars, so what's an age gap? If he's willing to pay for some nooky, who am I to judge? A mother superior really shouldn't judge others.

"Listen, I'm supposed to be meeting this guy-"

"I took care of it. You can meet with me instead. If you want to. If not, I can leave. . ."

"No! Fuck no. Please come inside."

"It's going to cost you," I barter.

"Baby, whatever you want, it's yours."

51

Whatever I want?

That's a dangerous promise.

"Two grand for an hour," I tell him.

"I'll give you ten to stay the night," he rejoins, and I almost fall over.

Fuck.

Me.

That's eight grand I could pocket for myself.

But how can I be gone all night?

That's definitely something a mother superior wouldn't do.

"I want the money upfront," my mouth speaks before my brain agrees.

The boy shrugs and invites me in. He takes me to his room and goes over to a safe, taking out ten thousand dollars. I make sure my expression is blank when I take the money and slip inside my satchel. Then, I turn back to Philip, a plan forming in my head.

I'm going to rock this kid's world, and to celebrate, we need drinks.

I fuck Philip six ways to Sunday.

And damn, does youth make him randy as hell.

Each time he comes, I pour him a shot and smoke a cigarette.

I'm in whore heaven.

I've been jonesing for a smoke in the worst way.

I'm on my fourth one when Philip finally passes out. It's nearly midnight. I take the rest of the pack and split the same way I did the night before: without a backward glance. When I get back to the convent, all the sisters are still up and waiting.

"How did your prayer circle go?" Sister Bernadette asks in concern.

I smile benignly and slyly answer, "It was great. Everyone *came.*"

Chapter 6

Forgive Me, Lord, I'm About to Sin

The next day, the sisters and I go out into the community, helping at a local food pantry and assisting those in need. I have to admit, everything that I've done so far has been very rewarding. I feel needed. People respect me and actually value my words, my opinions.

Me.

It's sad that I've had to lie, cheat, and steal to get here, but whatever.

That afternoon, after I deposited the money into the convent's bank account, I call Sister Mary-Francis in.

"I have great news; the diocese has decided that you can continue your education! They've already transferred the money and you are to sign-up immediately."

She stares at me in shock, then rounds the desk, sobbing, and throws her arms around me.

"Thank you, Mother Evangeline, thank you!"

Warmth spreads through my chest as I hug her back.

This lie and the price it took to do it: *fucking worth it.*

Worth it times a thousand.

I don't have a care in the world until Sister Rachel tells me that Father McMann is waiting for me in the chapel and that it's urgent.

My knees shake as I make my way outside and over to the chapel.

Has Father McMann learned my secret?

Does he know where I was last night?

Oh shit, oh shit, oh shit, I chant.

I try to think of a plausible lie for all of it, but my brain comes up with nothing.

I guess it's just time to face the music.

Taking a deep breath, I slap a serene look on my face and glide into the chapel.

"*Sweet Mother of God,*" I gasp when I see the vision before me. Belatedly, I realize how inappropriate my words are and quickly tack on a fake prayer. "Thank you for your immaculate heart. Amen."

I sketch a hasty sign of the cross and try not to stare at the men before me.

"Ah, Mother Evangeline!" Father McMann calls, coming from behind the altar. "I have a favor to ask. These lads are mentees of mine and will soon take their vows, but until then, could they stay at the convent? I simply don't have room at the rectory."

The convent has extra rooms in case those in need from the community are seeking shelter, so there definitely is enough space, but I can't even form a response. My tongue is glued to the roof of my mouth in shock. The four men before me are dressed in the familiar black slacks and shirt of a priest, but without the clerical collar.

They are easily all over six feet and fucking *gorgeous.*

Like, male-model gorgeous.

The fact that they plan to become priests is enough to make me weep for all of womanhood.

They shouldn't be swearing celibacy or spreading the word of God.

They would better serve humanity if they were spreading legs instead.

Namely *mine.*

"Mother, meet the Gospel Brothers," Father McMann chuckles at the name. "This is Matthew, Mark, Luke, and John."

I've got to stop gawking.

Nuns do *not* check out men, no matter how hot they are.

I clear my throat and finger the cross around my neck nervously.

"It's nice to meet you all. I'm Mother Evangeline. And of course, Father, anyone is welcome at the convent, but is it. . . ah, seemly, to have men staying under its roof for an extended period of time?"

I'm questioning more for my sanity than for any true interest in propriety.

If these men all sleep under the same roof as me for an indeterminant amount of time, there's no saying what I'll do.

The four of them could tempt a saint, and I'm so far from that status, it's not even funny.

I should probably just make a mental confession to God now: *Forgive me. I'm going to sin with these men. Over and over and over. Amen.*

Father McMann waves a hand.

"Perhaps at another convent, but not here. We're more laid back and practical. I simply don't have the space. Besides, they've offered to help fix up some of the things that need to be repaired and they will help in the community, too. Not to mention, they will be in the guest rooms on the first floor. All of the sisters' rooms and yours are on the second floor, preserving your modesty and privacy."

"Super. That is just. . . super. Um, ok, I'll just go tell the sisters, I guess."

"If it's not an inconvenience, you can take them over now and introduce them to everyone. I'm an old man and I get tuckered out fast," Father McMann jokes.

Mark, I think, slaps him on the back.

"Does that mean you won't be running with us in the morning?"

Father McMann grimaces.

"Do you still get up at four and jog five miles?"

Now I grimace.

Five miles?!

No wonder they are built like freaking Greek gods.

"No, we get up at five now and run six instead."

Both Father and I shake our heads at the insanity while the four men laugh.

"Good-night everyone. God bless," Father says, dismissing us, and I lead The Gospel Brothers to the convent.

I try to think of something to say, some kind of small talk, but all I can think about is us all having sex.

If I'm the Mother Superior and they screw me, does that make them *motherfuckers?*

"Before we go in, I really didn't catch who was who when Father introduced you all. Can you please tell me?" I ask instead of the real question inside my head.

"I'm Mark," one of the four confirms.

He seems to be the unspoken leader with wavy brown hair, warm brown eyes, and glowing tanned skin.

"I'm John, but I prefer Jay," the shortest of the bunch says.

And by shortest, I mean like six foot three.

He's basically a foot taller than my five foot four frame.

Jay is the golden boy of the group with short blond hair and light blue eyes.

His coloring reminds me of Walker, but there's a gentleness, a kindness even, in his eyes that Walker lacked.

"I'm Matthew," the second tallest calls out.

His hair is a sandy brown and his eyes are a hazel green.

That leaves only Luke, the tallest. His eyes are a striking blue against the dark fringe of his lashes and hair. He sees that I've made the connection and merely tips his head in acknowledgment.

This one is shy, I note.

"Great, thanks for clarifying. Listen, it's late and I've got to get to my prayers. So many prayers and so little time, right?" I joke nervously. "I can show you to your rooms and introduce you to the sisters tomorrow."

"Thank you. We greatly appreciate your hospitality," Mark says sincerely in a deep velvety voice.

I smile wanly, my knees a little weak.

61

God, I need a cigarette.

I show the four men to their rooms and then I race up to mine.

It's Mother Catherine's room.

Trust me, I balked when I learned that I would be sleeping in a bed that someone died in, but Father McMann blessed it.

Cue my eye roll.

Waving your hand over a bed doesn't cleanse it of bad juju, but I made my peace with it.

After ten minutes of searching, I come to the depressing conclusion that there's nothing in the room I can use to pleasure myself with.

I guess my hands are on manual labor duty tonight.

I can't remember ever being so horny.

And for a bunch of all-most priests, too!

I cringe.

I'm fucking racking up my years in Hell.

At this rate, all my future reincarnations will be going there, too, but the fantasy of those four men each having a go at me is too hot to ignore.

My evening with Philip yesterday was pleasurable enough, but only because I did the work.

I mean, I guess if I were paying someone to fuck me, I wouldn't work to get them off either, but still.

Now, I'm a horny mess.

It doesn't take much, just the thought of riding Mark's cock, before I explode around my fingers.

Phew, I'm glad that I got that out of my system. Tomorrow is a new day and I can focus on being a better nun. One without impure thoughts.

Yep.

Starting tomorrow.

Chapter 7

For the Love of God

Tomorrow comes too soon. I need more time to get them out of my system and my head, but duty calls.

Before morning mass, I call all the sisters into the community room and introduce the four novitiates. That's a fancy word that I learned last night, thanks to the internet. It means someone who hasn't taken their final vows yet. Man, I am killing it at this nunning stuff.

I'm pleased to note my fellow sisters wear the same dazed look on their faces when they meet The Gospel Brothers.

I'm totally not a sinner.

If anything, this is God's fault for making them too good-looking.

Shame on you, Big Guy.

There's a lot of blushing and stammering, but the guys seem oblivious. Maybe they don't realize their effect on women. I clear my throat and this gets the sisters' attention.

"Shall we go to mass, everyone?" I say piously, wondering if their dicks are as big as I imagine.

Afterward, Mark walks next to me back to the convent.

"What did you think of Father's homily?"

I blink at him blankly.

I couldn't tell you what Father McMann said on a normal day, let alone one where I spent the entire time fantasizing about their cock sizes.

"I agree with him," I respond because agreeing with a priest seems like common sense.

Also because 'it was very hommy' didn't sound right.

Mark gives me a funny look and I wonder if I fucked up.

"I do, too," he says, surprising me. "I think there are more interpretations to love. Just like how in the Bible, God created a woman from man to be his companion and decrees that they be fruitful and multiply, but this doesn't mean there's not room for other types of relationships. Rather,

66

they were simply not expounded upon. The authors didn't clarify everything because they probably didn't think people would take it literally and nitpick every other sentence."

"Yeah, well, love is love, right? What does it matter who's doing it or how?"

"True. Although the Bible is pretty clear about certain relationships, such as Sodom and Gomorrah."

I remember that tale from my youth.

"Maybe the point of the story wasn't so much about the type of sex as it was about promiscuity in general, but everyone got all butthurt about it and took it too literally," I offer.

Mark stops and stares at me.

Then he busts up laughing.

"Butthurt?" he chokes out and I wrinkle my nose.

Yeah, that might not be a word that a nun would use, especially when talking about sodomy.

"Sister Mary-Francis said you had a brazen sense of humor," Mark teases.

I shrug, blushing at his compliment.

I mean, it might not have been one, but I was taking it as one.

"I don't think God would have given us sexuality if we weren't meant to embrace it," I try to explain.

I'm not dumb, but I feel foolish whenever I speak religiously, like I'm just talking out of my ass. Which I pretty much am, but the sisters always seem interested to hear my unorthodox thoughts. Father McMann is pretty unorthodox himself.

Maybe that's why we all got along.

I focus back on Mark, who's talking again.

"The guys and I are going to the Y to help coach some basketball. If you or the sisters want to come help, we would appreciate the extra set of hands."

I look down at his hands and imagine him with an extra set.

Two-hands Mark is a god in my head, but Four-hands Mark?

A fucking demon in the fantasy sack.

"Yeah, I'll ask them."

If their looks this morning were any indication, then I'm sure they would all love to give a helping hand. But surprisingly, all the sisters declined. Either they hated basketball or they knew when to avoid temptation. I didn't, though. I had handed temptation my tainted soul a long time ago. It could call me up anytime. The naughtier, the better.

And it really didn't get any naughtier than daydreaming about four men of the cloth.

I help Sister Agnes with some office work before I make my way down to the YMCA. It's only a few blocks from the convent. When I get there, I can see kids already playing on the outside court. As I get closer, I see some adults there, too. Four, in particular, stand out.

Not because they are dressed like priests.

But because they *aren't* dressed like priests.

All four are wearing mesh shorts, but Luke and Jay are in tank tops that show off their bulging bicep muscles, and Matt and Mark are in tight t-shirts that showcase their abs. Praise Jesus the sisters stayed home. The temptation is too great for them to bear.

Fuck.

The temptation is too great for *me* to bear.

I wheel around to walk back to The Immaculate Heart of Mary when Jay calls out for me.

"Mother Evangeline! You came! Come join us."

I scowl.

I didn't come like I wanted to, but I did show up and it would be rude for me to leave now that they knew I was here. I step into the sunny courtyard and over to where everyone is waiting.

"I'm not very good at basketball," I admit.

"No big deal, you can help with drills," Matt says and he takes me to the side where kids are lined up.

He explains what I need to do and I try to listen.

I really do.

But I can't hear him over his abs. They are practically screaming at me to lick them.

Stop it, Abs!

I'm a good girl now.

Not really, but I need to pretend to be.

I also need to quit lying to myself. It's not healthy.

I really need to get that shit under control before I don't even believe myself.

"Got it?" Matt asks.

"Got it," I parrot, lying some more, but not to myself, so that's an improvement, right?

I figure out what I need to do through some trial and error. Eventually, all the younger kids cycle through my line and join the older kids and The Gospel Brothers on the main court to play. Mark beckons me over. I probably shouldn't, but I've already come this far, what's a little further?

Bad choice.

It was a bad choice.

Basketball is a contact sport.

Did you know that?

I sure as shit didn't, but I fucking learned today.

Gah, my lady bits are still a puddly mess of pheromones and need just thinking about Mark guarding my back, rubbing his fine-ass chest against it. Or when Luke swiped the ball from me but got a handful of my tit instead.

If someone had told me playing a sport was foreplay, I would have laughed in their faces.

Not after today.

That shit is sensuality in motion.

I call time and step over into the shadow of a tree. I need a break. Basketball is now officially the Gateway to Sex and Sin. It's making me hot, sweaty, and bothered as fuck. I plop down to the ground and Luke comes over, silently handing me a water bottle. I thank him and he nods. The other three join us and Mark yells at the kids to just have fun.

I watch as they start up their games.

I run a hand across my forehead and it comes back dripping.

Ew.

I yank off my veil, and it snags my bun, yanking it from its tight confines. My hair erupts and cascades down my back and shoulders in riotous curls, the sun making it glow a golden brown.

"Goddammit," I curse without thinking.

A choking sound draws my attention and I remember my company.

All four men are looking at me like I'm an alien who just landed in front of them.

Shit.

Is it because I just said like the worst swear word in nunhood, or is it my hair?

Are nuns not allowed to take off their headdresses in public?

Is flashing your hair unacceptable, like flashing your boobs when it isn't Mardi Gras?

Argh, I don't know!

I quickly mutter my apology, attempting to put back on the stifling headdress while promising to do a penance for swearing. Then, I run into the YMCA for some air conditioning and a judgment-free atmosphere.

Chapter 8

Basketball Boners

Well, the good news is that I got my air conditioning.

The bad news: it doesn't come with a judgment-free atmosphere.

I get inside and no sooner do I right my veil, than I feel a hand on my shoulder, spinning me around. But it's not one of my four handsome No-nos. It's some kid.

Some kid I *know*.

And he knows me.

"Raelynn?"

"Hey, Spencer," I say shakily.

Spencer's older brother sometimes does errands for The Outcasts of Hell. His family lives near the complex and even though Spencer is eleven, that's old enough to know how the world works. In our world, you're born knowing; there's no place for innocence.

"You know Walker is looking for you?"

It's a rhetorical question.

We both know Walker is looking for me and what he'll do when he finds me.

"Remember that time my sister got sick and you got her the medicine? And you said that it was our little secret because it could get you into a lot of trouble?"

I remembered.

It was the first time that I stole from Walker. I took the money and got Spencer's sister the meds she needed. Spencer's mom swears I saved her daughter's life, but I don't think it's as dramatic as all that.

"Yeah, I remember."

"Well, this can be our little secret, too," he shrugs and I narrow my eyes.

People don't do shit for free.

Spencer wants it to seem like this is in exchange for helping his sister way back when, but I can see the cunning in his eyes.

They're shifty and calculating.

"What do you really want, Spencer?" I demand.

"My brother Denny stabbed someone. He needs a place to hide. . ."

"Ugh, you've got to be kidding me?! You want me to give him sanctuary?"

We both know Denny isn't hiding from the cops.

"It's not safe for my sisters," I hedge.

"*Your sisters?* Are you really a nun now?"

"That's '*nun*' of your business," I tell him tartly.

There's a pause and then we both bust up at my terrible pun.

"Fine," I acquiesce, more to help him than to save my ass. "But only for a little bit. I really don't want to bring anything dangerous to the convent. The women there are good. Nice. . ."

"You don't need to explain it, Rae. They aren't like us. They deserve to live."

He says it simply. For him, he's just stating a fact, but it breaks my heart that he already lumps himself in with the bad guys. In our world, there's a clear demarcation. There's good, and there's bad. If you were born into the bad, that's just your lot in life. You'll never be good. You'll never not be tainted by the fucked up things that happen in a bad world.

You can run from it.

But you can't hide from it.

Not even behind a holy headdress.

"I'm staying at The Immaculate Heart of Mary. Send Denny there, but tell him he can only stay for a few days. He should make arrangements to leave the state. Depending on who he stabbed, maybe the country."

"He definitely needs to leave the country," Spencer confirms and I grimace.

Fuck, who the hell did Denny stab?

I don't want to know.

Ignorance truly is bliss.

Knowledge like this can get you killed.

I sigh.

"I'm going before I change my mind," I tell Spencer.

"Yeah, your boyfriends are probably waiting."

I stare at the kid in horror.

"What?" I splutter.

"Your boyfriends or whatever they are. Man, Walker would be pissed if he-"

"They aren't my boyfriends," I correct sternly. "They are priests. Practically. They're taking vows of celibacy, for fuck's sake."

"What's celibacy?"

"When you don't have sex."

"So you can make out?"

"Erm, I'm not sure where they draw the line."

"You should ask because I'm pretty sure they want to make out with you," Spencer states matter-of-factly.

"What makes you say that?" I wonder.

Spencer scoffs at my naiveté.

"They all had boners playing basketball with you."

I choke trying to swallow, which is a first for me.

I swallow like a fucking champ.

"You shouldn't know what a boner is," I chide.

"I have a dick, Rae. I know about boners and sex."

I cover my ears.

"Lalalala, not listening!"

Spencer laughs at my childish antics as he walks away, and the sound warms my heart. This is how an eleven-year-old should sound, not talking about cock and what to do with it. I head back outside into the bright sunshine. All the kids are gone and the guys seem to be waiting for me. I give an awkward little wave, trying to look everywhere but at their penises.

"I should, ah, explain," I begin. "The last convent I was at, we did a lot of. . . um, manual labor. Like Habit for Humanity or some shi- stuff, but for nuns. It was impractical to wear a habit or a veil."

Matthew nods his head in understanding and it draws my attention to his dick.

That's another lie.

I was totally eyeing his cock before this. I can make out the outline through his black, mesh shorts and the length alone has my mouth watering.

"The work was hard, so very hard," I hear myself continue, "and it made me wet."

Matt's dick twitches at my words.

"Sweaty!" I hastily correct. "It made me sweaty, so it was just better if I had nothing on at all."

80

Now, he groans.

Jesus needs to come shut me up, but he left this conversation a long time ago.

"I don't mean I was naked," I clarify. "I'm never naked. Nuns don't get naked. Wait, that's not true. We get naked to shower. Or at least I'm naked when I shower. Crap, was I supposed to be wearing a suit or something this entire time? How am I supposed to clean my vagina if it's covered? Like, just rub the soap through the suit and hope it gets in there?"

I realize that I'm pantomiming rubbing non-existent soap into my pussy and Matt's dick is at full mast. Clearly, it salutes the visual of me washing myself. I stare at it like a starving person. And I am- starving for pork sword. Kosher, holy, pork sword.

Wow, something's wrong with me.

Matt clears his throat, and I realize that my eyes haven't left his impressive erection. When I make eye-contact with him again, I notice his cheeks are bright pink. Probably because a nun is checking out his junk. Which is totally something a nun *wouldn't* do. I quickly slap a hand over my eyes and pretend to be embarrassed.

Then, I part my fingers so I can keep staring.

81

It seems like such a waste not to look at it since no one will be riding it to glory.

The silence stretches on between the five us and I decide that I need to do something nunly.

I clear my throat.

"You know, that saying 'out like a boner in sweatpants' suddenly makes sense now."

Crickets.

Maybe I need to give some motherly advice instead.

"Why don't you just tuck it into your waistband. It'll hide it and it feels good."

I drop my hand to see all four men gaping at me, and I scowl. This is all *their* faults. What are they thinking, wearing clothes like this and tempting someone of my respectable position? I bite my lip and paste a virtuous look on my face.

"If you gentlemen will excuse me, I must go pray."

With that, I beat a hasty retreat back to the convent.

I'm going to pray for my soul.

And their souls.

And Matt's boner's soul.

82

May it find heaven inside of me.

Chapter 9

Not Today, Jesus

I roll over and look at the clock.

1:13 in the morning.

Ugh.

I can't sleep. I'm so fucking horny, it's not even funny. The tent that Matt pitched in his pants keeps dancing in my head whenever I close my eyes. I grin when I remember his red face. The things I could do to that man would make his head spin. And just thinking about all the things I could teach him to do to me. . .

The blush would never leave his cheeks.

I need to stop thinking with my pussy; she's a needy See You Next Tuesday.

What I really need to do is pray for her.

My vag needs the Holy Spirit in her life.

Dear God, it's me. Fake Mother Evangeline. Please send down your Holy Spirit to fill me up with his heavenly cucumber. May it marinate inside of me until I pickle his ghostly pecker. Amen.

Huh, that's one of my better prayers that I've come up with.

Better than just screaming 'Oh, God' like I have been doing in my head.

It's muffled because my face is shoved into the bed, and Matt is working my ass just right.

I call it 'fantasy praying'.

I sigh and roll over to get out of Mother Catherine's bed. I don't care if she's dead. It's still her bed. I'm just the imposter who's sleeping in it, fantasizing about four priests-to-be. I need to work off this sexual energy. I'm out of cigarettes and my fingers aren't doing the job well enough.

I need some real dick or a stiff replacement.

But where the hell am I going to get either of those at this hour, inside a house of chaste women?

Maybe they had an old-fashioned washer and dryer.

I could sit on it and get off to the good vibrations.

I tug on a habit, but I don't even bother with the headdress. I sneak down to the main floor and then to the basement, where the kitchen and community room are located. I find the closet with the washer and dryer, but it's a sleek upright number, with the dryer stacked on top of the washer.

I slam the door in frustration.

I might as well get a snack while I'm down here. I snoop around the pantry and find those little wafer things that they serve at communion. Oh, and the communal wine. That's this cult's Kool-Aid. I can work with it, though. Apparently, it's supposed to be the blood of Christ. . .

Gross, right?

We're supposed to drink this holy dude's blood.

Makes you wonder: are Catholics closet-vampires?

Or is it the other way around, and Jesus' blood is wine?

If that's the case, Jesus must have been wasted as fuck, twenty-four seven. No wonder everyone loves him. I bet he was a fun guy. I could totally see Jesus and I partying together at Mardi Gras. We could share my beads from all the tittie it's ok to flash on this joyous holiday.

87

I look down and realize I've drank half the bottle of wine and two sleeves of Christ's body.

Christ's *motherfucking body.*

Not only are Catholics closet-vamps, they are also cannibals.

As a Mother now, I'm finding a lot of disturbing things about this faith. But I'm not here to judge. I'm here to indulge my stomach. I would much prefer to indulge my pussy, but blasphemous liars can't be choosers.

Also, if I'm going to be honest, Christ's blood tastes delicious. Much better than his body. That's a little flat and bland. I drink down some more of the Lord's deliciousness and settle back in my chair. My belly is pleasantly full and sloshes a little when I move. I feel sleepy, but that damn ache between my legs is still there.

It won't go away and I can't ignore it.

I need something *in* me.

I walk over to another closet and open it to inspect its contents.

It's the cleaning closet.

There's a broom. . .

I'm desperate enough that might work.

I'm reaching for it when something else catches my eye: a floor buffer.

Bingo.

I drag the relic out and find an outlet. After I unravel the cord and plug it in, I straddle the front, riding the silver pole that runs between the machine and the handlebars. I pull my black habit up, exposing my naked ass, and flip the thing on.

Immediately, the room is filled with the gentle hum of the machine and my pussy throbs with the vibrations from it. I lean back a little and slide up and down the cold metal, rubbing my clit in the process. I hear myself moan and crack my eyes half open.

In front of me is a giant cross.

With a giant Jesus.

And I'll be damned if he's not giantly judging the fuck out of me right now.

I glare at him.

"Stop censoring me!" I slur to him. "Can't a nun 'bate in peace?"

Jesus doesn't say anything, but I swear his frown deepens.

That's it.

I turn off the floor polisher and lean forward to turn the massive crucifix over.

Christ can judge the wall; I'm getting off.

Satisfied that the statue can no longer see my movements, I return to pleasuring myself. I imagine the handles are Matt's shoulders as I ride him, his hazel eyes wide. Silent Luke is standing behind Matt and I'm sucking his dick like it's a popsicle made of holy water. Mark is behind me, DPing the shit out of me, and Jay is taking it all in, stroking his cock to my priest porn fantasy.

These fantasy Gospel Brothers are so bad, but still so innocent.

I can see the shock and desire on Matt's face when he comes inside someone for the first time. I can taste the desperate need of the others as they follow suit. A strangled moan escapes my mouth as I come for real. I fucking unleash on the floor buffer like it's my favorite lover, my juices dripping off the pole.

"*Mother?*" a shocked voice calls as the overhead lights flip on.

90

I freeze, the rounded globes of my ass still on display.

I slowly, and dizzily, turn my head to take in the four last men I had ever hoped to encounter in this situation. It was Luke who spoke, a testimony of how stunned the others are. I quickly turn off the floor buffer and swing my leg over to get off of it. Unfortunately, Jesus' blood is some potent shit and I fall over, knocking the cleaning machine into the giant cross.

It twists around and comes falling down on top of me, Christ's face right between my tits.

With a shriek of indignation, I shove him off and slap his face for motorboating me without my permission.

"Not today, Jesus!" I yell.

I look to others to make sure they were catching all this. My faux pas wasn't nearly as terrible as the Lord's. Hell, I'm convinced the only reason the holy pervert didn't cop a feel is because he couldn't. Not with his hands pinned down like that. Belatedly, I realize I'm mentally castigating a statue.

The statue is the pervert.

Not Jesus.

Forgive me, Lord.

Please still send down the Holy Spirit to fill me up.

I feel so empty and cold down there.

Wait.

That's just a draft because I'm sprawled on the ground with my legs spread-eagle, but still, send him to me.

Clearly, I need spiritual help.

Mark has come over and is holding out a hand to physically help me up.

I do us both a favor and tug hard when I grasp it. Mark doesn't expect this and tumbles forward, toppling to the ground, where I help him get comfortable by straddling his fine-ass abs. I rock a little because it feels so good and moan loudly. When I look down, Mark's pupils are blown and he's breathing erratically. My long, dark hair swings around us as I reach back and run a hand over his *very* hard dick. I whimper like a whore while I pet him.

Screw this.

I ditch stroking him in favor of tugging his sleep pants off.

I need to be righteously rodgered, right-the-fuck-now.

The movement makes my head swim, though, and I keel over. Mark uses this to scramble to his feet and the other three come over to join us. All four men wear matching frowns and remind me of Pervy-Statue-Jesus. Jay helps me to my feet and I lean into his chest for balance.

Mark takes a laboring, deep breath and exhales harshly.

"Are you *drunk?*" he demands.

"Yerp," I confirm. "Wasted on the blood of Christ. You should probably make me do some penance, or suck your dicks, or something. That'll learn me."

I pitch forward, but luckily, Jay tugs me back. I thank him by turning and hiking my long leg up. I hook it around his waist while staring deeply into his crystal-blue eyes. Then I lean in and kiss him. Every inch of his body tightens in response to my surprise kiss and he purses his lips into a thin line, but I'm undaunted.

I lick and nibble until he gasps, and then I slip my tongue inside and kiss him like I've dreamed. I grind my bared pussy against his soft sweatpants and find nirvana in his mouth. He tastes like peppermint and sweet forbiddance. I wonder if I taste like sex and sin is my last thought before the darkness takes over my mind.

Chapter 10

Divine Intervention

JAY

A million different thoughts and sensations assault me and I nearly collapse from the bombardment. Riding in the forefront of this tidal wave of emotion is desire, pure and simple. It licks up and down my body until I'm nothing but a trembling mass of need.

I stare down at the gorgeous beauty in my arms.

Her long curly hair is unbound and she's staring at me like a parched man who's finally found water. Her eyes are a turbulent blue mixed with green, the color standing out brightly against her olive-complected skin. Right now, they're clouded from having drank half a bottle of wine on her own.

I can see the evidence sitting on the table, next to some communion wafers.

95

Even more disturbing than her appearance is the way her body is entwined around mine.

It's my fault.

I never should have helped her up.

I should have let one of my brothers assist Mother Evangeline.

I'm the weakest link in our group.

The biggest sinner.

I try to concentrate on *anything* except the feel of her against me.

I pray; I beg; I plead.

Please, Lord, save me from this temptation. It's been eight months since I've touched myself. Eight months that I haven't thought of a woman in this way. Eight months. . .

My prayer fizzles inside my head when Mother Evangeline locks eyes with mine and rocks herself into me. It takes everything for me not to groan out loud. I can feel her heat searing me through my pajama pants and it feels good- *so good.*

For being drunk, Evangeline's eyes are alight with purpose and this makes me uneasy.

What is she thinking?

Suddenly, she leans in and *kisses* me.

All my muscles lock up in response and I stop breathing. Maybe if I don't move, she'll stop, but the woman is undaunted. She snakes out her tongue and I feel it sensuously trace my lips.

I gasp.

I can't help it.

And then her tongue fills my mouth and I stop thinking all together.

I just *feel.*

Her gentle rocking has become a fierce grind and her soft whimpers are my undoing. To my utter shame and embarrassment, I cup her behind, drawing her in closer, and explode. Eight months of pent up and repressed passion come spilling out, but still I keep kissing her.

Then I feel her small body sag, her leg going lax around my waist.

I realize she's passed out, and I barely catch her in the nick of time.

I look at Mark, who seems to be in much the same condition as me, sans the wet stain on the front of his sweats. Matt and Luke are behind me, but I can hear their choppy breaths.

Silently, I turn and hand Mother Evangeline off to Luke.

He's the most stoic and grounded of the four of us.

Why didn't I let him help Evangeline in the first place?

I catch Luke staring at the front of my pants and I burn with mortification.

How am I going to confess this to Father McMann?

LUKE

I reflexively clutch Mother Evangeline closer to my body when Jay passes her off. Her head lolls against my chest, and I tuck it into the crook of my arm. Part of me is displeased that Jay handed her to me, but the other part is relieved.

It gives me something to focus on.

Anything but the front of Jay's pants, dark with the evidence of his release.

Of course, Mother Evangeline is no better of a distraction.

The woman is stunning with her veil on, but without it, the absolute perfection of her features is haloed by her glorious hair and she's simply breathtaking. I settle on closing my eyes and breathing deeply, clearing my head of the inappropriate thoughts that have taken hold of me.

I focus instead on neutralizing my irritation.

At Jay.

At Mother Evangeline.

At myself.

Everyone thinks that I'm this rock, this dispassionate and stalwart man.

Over time, the people in my life have equated it to controlled and emotionless, but just because I keep my feelings contained doesn't mean that I don't have any.

Or that I feel them any less.

I burn with them and fight every day not to let them consume me, body and soul.

And now I'm scared.

The flame that I had thought I snuffed so long ago has come back to life.

And Mother Evangeline lit the match.

No one speaks.

Although, what is there to say?

Luke has his eyes closed, like he can shut the scene from his memory, but I doubt it.

This will be permanently etched there; it will be permanently etched in all our minds.

I try to concentrate on the task at hand.

As the oldest, the others generally defer to my judgement, but we're a team. We are going to work through this together.

I clear my throat.

Once.

Twice.

I can't seem to get the image of Mother Evangeline on top of me out of my head.

I've never felt anything so soft and feminine before.

"Ugh," I groan, swiping a hand down my face in frustration.

The sound and movement seem to break the spell of silence and Matt walks over, clapping a supportive hand on my shoulder.

"You ok, Mark?"

"No. Are any of us ok from this?"

No one answers my rhetorical question. The pained look on all their faces is answer enough.

"What should we do?" Jay wonders in a tortured whisper and I wince at the desperation that I hear in it.

"John," I use his whole name to get his attention, "it's going to be ok. We're going to work through this."

Everyone knows what I'm talking about. Jay has a weakness for the sins of the flesh. Since entering the priesthood, he has been able to contain his urges to self-pleasure, but I know it's been a long time since he's indulged.

A very long time, if the size of the stain on his pants is accurate, but I have no room to talk. If Mother Evangeline hadn't pitched herself sideways off my body, who knows what might have happened. I probably would be in the same shape as Jay, or worse.

"She needs help," I finally manage.

My brothers and I are no strangers to temptations. Many brothers and sisters struggle with different types of addiction. Apparently, Mother Evangeline has at least two vices: drinking and sex. She just needs someone to help guide her back.

"What are you saying?" Matt asks.

"She's lost her way. She needs help finding her true path again. We can intervene."

Jay snorts.

"*We* can intervene? She needs divine intervention, not ours. We're the last people who should help her," he rejoins.

Luke and Matt nod.

"We can help her," I insist. "We are strong enough."

"Really?" Jay asks sarcastically, sweeping a hand towards his groin.

Luke quickly closes his eyes again.

"Really," I say firmly. "We are not turning our backs on someone in need."

We need to prove that we can do this, and not just for Mother Evangeline, *but for ourselves.*

Out of the four of us, I seem to be in the best shape compared to my brothers.

Of course, this isn't because I'm better than them.

In fact, it's the exact opposite: because I'm a sinner.

Earlier, when we had returned to the convent, I had excused myself to go to the chapel. I said that I needed to pray.

And I did.

I needed to get on my knees and beseech God to take the images of Mother Evangeline from my mind.

Everything was seared in my head.

The sight of her hair tumbling out of her veil, glinting in the sun.

Or worse, the insidious feel of her underneath me when we played basketball.

I've played sports with fellow brothers and sisters and I can honestly say that I've never had a sexual reaction to another nun before.

Although, Mother Evangeline is no ordinary nun.

She's an angel.

Truly one of the most beautiful women I've ever seen.

So while I had every intention of praying when I entered the peaceful chapel, I ended up stroking myself to the mental sight, feel, scent, sound, and taste of the forbidden woman.

Twice.

Now, my lapse into sin seems all for naught because when Mark said he heard something in the basement and we all went to investigate, the sight of Mother Evangeline getting off had my mind, and dick, right back to square one.

At the time, I had been angled behind all my brothers, and I swiftly shifted inside my pants to bring my erection up against my stomach.

Mother Evangeline might need our help, but she was right about one thing: tucking my boner into my waistband hid it and it *did* feel good.

Chapter 11

Call Me Mommy

Incessant pounding is what wakes me up.

I roll over, confused.

Where am I?

The holy faces of various saints swim into view and I realize that I'm in Mother Catherine's room again.

It takes me a minute, but everything from the night before comes rushing back with sickening clarity.

Why the fuck couldn't I have just forgotten everything?!

Then I could pretend it never happened.

"Who is it?" I finally manage to croak when the knocking doesn't stop.

"It's us, Mother," one of the sisters calls.

Sister María Concepción, I think.

"Come in," I finally yell, wondering if this is a mistake.

The door opens and in march my sisters, the women that I've known for less than two weeks, but to whom I've grown very fond.

Sister Rachel is carrying a tray and I can smell something delicious.

"Father McMann said the brothers mentioned you were ill. We are going with him to help teach some catechism classes at another parish that is understaffed. We'll be back tonight, but one of us can stay with you, if you would prefer," the sweet nun offers.

"No, thank you. I appreciate your offer, but I think that I will spend the day praying and recovering."

"As you wish, Mother."

The women all hug me good-bye and hope that I feel better soon.

"Oh, Mother, I almost forgot," Sister Agnes suddenly exclaims. "Someone came by seeking refuge under our roof. He says that he knows you and that you offered for him to stay. . ."

Shit.

I had forgotten about Denny.

"Um, yes. A troubled young lad? Tattoos up and down his arms?"

"That's the one," Sister Agnes confirms.

"I will go and speak with him when I am feeling better to see that he is settled. I told him that he could only stay for a few days because I wasn't sure of your policy here," I rush to add on.

"He is welcome as long as needed, Mother. We have no policy, but serve children first and foremost. God has a plan for each of us and sometimes it takes others to help us see it unfold. Perhaps Denny simply needs our guidance to reach his full potential."

I smile at her charming naivety.

Denny doesn't need our guidance.

Depending on who he stabbed, he needs a fucking miracle.

But it's not my problem- and it better stay that way.

It's risky bringing him here, but no more dangerous than me hiding here, as well. I can't pretend otherwise or else I would be a hypocrite.

109

Besides, I have bigger fish to fry.

Like why didn't the brothers rat me out to Father McMann and the other nuns?

What are they up to?

I eat my soup thoughtfully, trying to guess their motives.

I come up with diddly squat.

I just need to confront them.

I get dressed in a white habit today, it makes me feel more devout and motherly.

First, I go find Denny.

He's in the first vacant room, lying on the bed, scrolling through his phone. He startles when he sees me in the door, squinting hard.

"You really became a fucking nun?" he asks incredulously.

"Hey! Watch your mouth! This is a House of God, for fuck's sake," I scold, completely contradicting myself. "And yes, I am a nun now. Mother Evangeline is what you must call me."

"Mother? Like you're my mommy? I didn't know nuns were into that shit. Will you call me *daddy*?" he smirks, waggling his eyebrows at me.

I smack one tattooed arm.

"Absolutely not. Now, who did you stab?"

"I'm not telling you," he says, becoming very solemn.

"That bad?" I grimace.

"Enough to get you killed for harboring me."

"Well, the Outcasts of Hell already want me dead, so I doubt one more person is much of a threat. . ."

"It was Cancer," Denny blurts out.

"WHAT?!" I screech.

Cancer is the VP of the Outcasts of Hell and Walker's first cousin. Walker and he go way back, long before they were even club members. They are practically brothers.

"Why in the fuck did you stab Cancer?" I breathe.

"Because. . ."

"*Because*," I prompt.

"Because Cancer fucking deserved to die."

I snort.

It's kind of funny when he says that because *all* cancer needs to die, but so does this piece-of-shit.

"Care to elaborate?" I drawl.

Denny huffs.

"I was seeing his girl behind his back, if you must know, and he found out. The fucker was going to kill her, so I knew that I had to kill him first. Except I didn't."

"Oh my god," I murmur. "How could you be so fucking stupid?"

"Says the girl who was stealing from Walker."

I wince.

Did everyone know about that?

"Alright, alright. I get your point. Damn, we are in some shit. Spencer is right; you need to get out of the country."

"So do you," he counters.

"Yes, I'm biding my time though. No one would ever think to look for me here. What. . . what happened to your girl?"

Denny looks down.

112

"I don't know. We ran separate ways."

A chill runs down my spine.

"Ok, listen. I told the other nuns that you'll be staying here for a few days, but you really need to get somewhere safer. My advice: don't leave this fucking convent."

"Didn't plan to. I'm just going to sit in here and chill. You got a TV or something for me?"

"No. This is a convent, not a freaking Motel 6."

"Well, you got anything I could read at least?"

"There's a Bible in your nightstand," I offer.

"What the hell am I supposed to do with that?" he snarks.

"Read it," I spit right back. "Study it; learn from it. Now, I have to go. I have things to do. Behave yourself."

"Yes, *mommy*," he replies sarcastically and I glare at him.

I turn to sweep out of the room and a pack of cigarettes catches my eye.

Jackpot.

"Oh, and I will be confiscating these. There's no smoking on the premises."

"But-"

I slam the door on his objection and walk off into the Reflection Garden.

A smoke is just what I need.

Chapter 12

Stop, Drop, and Pray

With my back against the towering privacy fence, I lean back and take a drag from a much-needed cigarette. I lazily blow Os in the air and contemplate my next move. Like Denny said, I need to get out of this country, too, but how? I don't have connections now.

Fuck, I don't even have any identification.

I'm a pretend nun.

Ugh.

I close my eyes and just enjoy my smoke.

There's only six cigarettes in the pack, so I better make them last and enjoy each and every one of them.

Someone clears their throat and I pop an eye open, a glare already forming.

Denny, that fuck-

I gasp.

Not Denny.

The Gospel Brothers.

I seriously had forgotten about them.

Sort of.

 Mark is staring at me sternly.

I frown back and he looks pointedly at my cigarette.

Oh, right.

Nuns probably didn't smoke.

I quickly toss it behind me and grab my rosary.

"Gentlemen, I can't talk right now. I'm in the middle of praying."

"We need to speak, Mother Evangeline," Mark insists stubbornly.

He's still calling me *Mother?*

"We know that you've fallen from the path of righteousness. . ."

His words remind me of *The Emperor's New Groove.*

"That's because I'm on the path that rocks," I quote Devil Kronk.

When you spend your time hiding in a room with internet access, you watch strange and sad shit. And if Walker ever checked his internet history, he would know that I'm a huge Disney fan.

Mark's face looks like it's been carved in stone.

"We are going to help you back to your true calling," he announces tightly, and I squint at him.

Oh Lord, he thinks I'm just some lost little nun sheep. He doesn't suspect that I'm in disguise.

"Listen, brother, I appreciate-"

I stop, sniffing.

"Do you guys smell that?"

For the first time, Luke, Jay, and Matt make eye-contact with me. Only Mark has been brave enough to do so up until this point. They sniff the air, their noses crinkling when the acrid smell of something burning hits them. I keep inhaling, searching for the cause, when a light catches my eye.

I swivel around in horror to see my pristine white habit ablaze from the cigarette I'd thrown behind me.

"Ah!" I shriek in dismay, getting up to run away.

Which is stupid, since I'm attached to the damn thing.

I run in circles, flapping about in panic, while the guys try to catch me without setting themselves on fire.

"Oh, God! Oh, God! Oh, God!"

"Stop praying and start rolling!" Mark roars.

"What?!" I screech back.

"STOP, DROP, AND ROLL!"

The drill mandated to us in elementary school comes rushing back and I throw myself onto the dirt path and roll around to tamp out the flames. I cry out in pain when the smoldering fabric hits my skin and I somehow manage to yank the thing off.

I quickly stand up and jump away from the material like it might follow me.

The four guys surround me, trying to soothe and calm me down.

"I'll bring her some clothes," Luke announces and strides off.

I realize that I'm just standing there in my lacy bra and thong and I try to cover myself with my hands, which does nothing but draw more attention to my nudity. But the guys don't seem to be caught up on my near nakedness; instead, their eyes are snagged on my tattoos.

Well, Matt's eyes are.

Mark and Jay are staring at something even worse.

My brand.

I self-consciously cover the circle with my palm, feeling the raised and divotted flesh underneath.

Luke comes back in record time with a simple t-shirt and some sweats. I hastily pull everything on, but I feel their gazes burning into me, searing me hotter than the flames that burned my habit. When I finish, I look back up and catch Mark assessing me critically.

The look unnerves me.

His golden-brown eyes consider me knowingly.

"I think we should pray together," he abruptly declares, startling me with his words.

"Erm, okay."

"Come, sit with me on the bench. We must thank the Lord for your miraculous save. Not an inch of you was burned. Surely, the Lord sent his angels to watch over you.

I think the Nicene Creed is the perfect prayer to offer up to him for his magnitude."

I look at him cautiously, trying to figure out his game.

"I think an Our Father would be better," I counter. "Or maybe a Hail Mary, since this is the home of her Immaculate Heart."

"How about all three?" Matt joins. "I think all three are perfect to express our thanks."

"Good point, brother," Mark says. "We'll start with the Our Father, as Mother Evangeline wanted."

We say the prayer, my words barely above a whisper, but Mark's eyes never leave my lips. And not because he finds them irresistible, but because he's *reading* them.

A shudder runs through me.

"Now the Nicene Creed," Mark directs.

I pitch my voice even lower and bow my had to hide my lips.

I don't know this prayer.

Usually, if I don't know a prayer, there's enough voices to drown out my ignorance, but with only five people, it's very obvious to hear my hesitation.

Or lack of knowledge.

It's even more obvious when four of the five people stop speaking and the fifth person is just mumbling.

"It's interesting, Mother Evangeline," Mark drawls when my pathetic attempt at reciting the prayer dwindles off, "The boy seeking refuge here. . .Denny, I believe? He has the same tattoo as you. Of course, his isn't *branded* into his skin. It makes you wonder why a nun and someone running from the law would have the same marks on their bodies?"

"How do you know he's hiding from the law?"

"Do I look stupid to you?" comes his acerbic rebuttal.

"He's not running from the law," I argue angrily.

"You think whoever put those marks on your bodies isn't the law?" Mark asks, somewhat softer. "Who are you?"

I open my mouth to lie.

"The truth!" Mark cuts me off fiercely before I can even begin.

I fold my hands together, trying to stifle the shaking that has consumed them.

"Answer me!" Mark barks and one of the other guys growl.

"Back off, Mark! Can't you see that she's scared?" Matt demands.

This time, Jay steps forward and looks deeply into my eyes.

"We can't help you if we don't know what's going on."

I want to tell them; I do, but it's dangerous.

Not only for myself, but for them.

"I'm Mother Evangeline," I tell them obstinately and Mark swears.

Actually swears.

"Dammit, I said don't lie to me, woman!"

"Stop yelling at me! Priests don't yell!" I scream at him because, apparently, it's acceptable for nuns to do so.

"You don't know the first thing about being a priest. Or a nun, for that matter."

"Bullshit! If that were the case, you would have questioned who I was long before now. Hell, up until you saw my brand, you just thought I had "fallen off the right path"," I air-quote.

"So you admit you aren't who you say you are!"

"No!"

I'm surprised that Denny hasn't come running to figure out what all the shouting is about.

"If you have no conscience whatsoever about impersonating a bride of Christ, at least have the decency to tell us what happened to the *real* Sister Evangeline!"

"How should I know?" I pretend.

"Please," comes Luke's soft, deep voice form behind me. "Please tell us so we can help her."

My shoulders slump in defeat.

"I'm sorry, Luke, you can't help her. She's already dead."

And then I break down and cry at the enormity of my lie.

Chapter 13

Sexy Mathematician

I feel strong, muscular arms wrap around me and pull me against an equally muscled chest.

"I've got you," comes Luke's reassuring voice.

Who knows how long I sit on the bench, sobbing into the tall and stoic man's black shirt. Eventually, my tears dry up and I feel lighter, but I know now they're expecting answers. I peek up through my wet lashes to find Matt sitting to my right; Jay and Mark are standing in front of us, their arms crossed over their chests.

"My name's not Evangeline," I mumble and Jay actually grins.

"We kind of guessed that," he teases. "How did the real one pass?"

"I didn't kill her!" I blurt in a rush.

All four men squint at me.

"Why would you think that we would think that?" Mark wonders.

I shrug.

"Because I'm obviously hiding something."

"Well, we know that you're not telling us the truth, but we certainly don't suspect you of *murder*," Matt offers.

I tip my head to assess the four men.

They know I'm lying, but seem hellbent on believing me.

No one has ever given me their explicit trust like this.

In my world, you have to earn it, and even if you achieve some level of confidence in a person, it's never one hundred percent.

Anyone can turn their back on you; it just depends on the price.

But these men don't have a price; they genuinely just want to help.

I haltingly tell them about the Outcasts of Hell, my story, and how Sister Evangeline saved me.

"I had every intention of telling the truth, but. . ."

"But survival came first," Jay supplies for me.

126

I nod.

I might have the shit lot in life, but I still am alive and I prefer to keep it that way.

"Did Sister Evangeline say anything else?" Jay continues.

"No- oh, wait! She mentioned another person was there. She told me to go with Gabrielle, but I swear there was no other sister there."

Matt cocks his head at my words and the others nod knowingly.

Weird.

"Well, for what it's worth, I'm glad you got out of there," Mark finally says.

His mouth twists in a grimace at his next words.

"I'm sorry that Walker thinks he owns you. You aren't a possession. You're a beautiful soul and deserved to be treated as such. That the man branded you like cattle and. . ."

"Whored her out," Jay finished Mark's sentence flatly. "Some guy urinated on her, for pity's sake."

Luke and Matt look simultaneously disgusted and affronted on my behalf.

"How did you get through that?" Matt wonders.

"Well, I try to stay positive, ya know? I always tell myself the guy could have shit on me instead."

One of the guys makes a gagging sound, and I giggle a little.

"But how did you convince everyone you're a nun?" Mark continues from earlier, ever tenacious on his quest for the whole truth and nothing but the truth, so help him God.

"Before Walker... I was in foster homes. One of them was a Christian home."

"Not Catholic?"

"I'm really not sure what denomination, but I don't think it was Catholic. That's why I know some of the prayers and rituals, but not all of them."

Marks nods, "That makes sense and explains why you didn't know the Nicene Creed. It's not used as widely in other Christian denominations and Catholics have a specific translation that others don't use."

Ugh, that damn prayer is what sold me out.

Sort of.

Not really, but I'm blaming it.

"Why did you pick *that* prayer?" I ask Mark resentfully. "Is it really about thanking God from saving your ass from burning?"

The four guys chuckle at my surly tone.

"Of course not. I don't think there is a specific prayer for, what did you call it? *Saving your ass from burning?*"

For some reason, hearing him swear makes me hot.

It reminds me that he's still just a man.

With manly urges.

"When I saw your brand, I knew something was amiss. I mean, after last night, I already suspected, but not at the level of you impersonating a nun. The brand gave you up. I figured I would pick one of the hardest prayers for you to recite. Most Catholics can't say it," he smirks and I glare at him for tricking me.

I register his words and look down at my lap again.

"About last night. . ."

"What about it?"

Matt's words make me jump.

129

"Um, not much. I just want to apologize. Things got way out of hand." I lower my voice to a whisper, "I mean, I sort of was even sexually assaulted by Jesus."

None of the four hold back at this and simply howl with laughter. I harrumph in indignation. It's not ok for Walker to do it, but since it's their Lord and Savior, he can get away with it? It's favoritism, I tell you, pure and simple.

"Are you going to tell Father McMann and the other sisters about me?" I ask worriedly, my mind bouncing back to the problem at hand.

"Let's see if we can't handle this amongst the five of us, first, ok?" Mark says and I relax.

"Ok."

Luke gives me a strange look.

"How long were you with Walker?"

I swallow.

"Nineteen long-ass years."

"How old are you now?" Jay wonders.

"Thirty-three."

All four men blink at me.

"What?" I ask, paranoid.

"Why were you with Walker at *fourteen?*" Matt demands to know.

Wow, someone is sexy and good at math.

"Because I ran away and Walker picked me up. In the beginning, he wasn't like he is now. This was before he became the MC's president. He was softer, then, I guess. I dunno."

"You ran away at fourteen?" Luke whispers.

I take a deep breath, hating the memories that come rushing back with his question.

"No, I ran away at thirteen," I manage to get out.

"Where did you live for that year?" Jay asks, the horror evident on his face.

"The streets," I answer flatly.

"Ok, I can see these questions bother you, but one more," Mark prods. "Why did you run away?"

I turn away from them now, trying to shut them and recollection of that time aside.

"Because no one believed me," I final choke out, still bitter twenty years later.

"Who didn't believe you?"

131

"Everyone," I murmur hatefully, but then I chuckle ruefully, turning back to the boys. "But who would believe a familyless nobody over my foster father, who was one of the most upstanding people in the parish?"

I get up to walk away.

I need to be alone for a while.

Jay catches my arm as I try to slink by.

"We believe you," he says solemnly.

"You don't even know what you're supposed to be believing," I snort.

"It doesn't matter," Luke speaks behind me.

"We'll always believe you," Matt vows.

My heart clenches.

Where have these men been all my life?

Chapter 14

Christ on a Cracker

That evening, all the sisters, the Gospel Brothers, and Father McMann have dinner in the basement together. Usually, we can't all sit down to sup because everyone has something going on outside in the community, but not tonight. I admit, being in this room again makes me uncomfortable. The feel of Mark's washboard abs and Jay's stiff cock dance in the edges of my mind, even as I try to banish them.

Plus, I'm even more nervous since the guys know my secret.

What if they change their mind and tell everyone?

What happens to someone who impersonates a nun?

Is it like impersonating a cop, but instead of the law directing you to jail, God just comes and escorts you to Hell?

I glower at my mushroom soup.

133

"Your smile's upside down, Mother," Sister Agatha teases me.

Sister Rachel looks worried.

"Do you not like the soup?" she asks in concern.

"Of course, I love it!" I quickly reassure her and she beams a smile.

"Good! Our guest didn't seem overly impressed with it. . ."

"Who?" I ask.

"Denny," Sister Patricia reminds me.

"Ah," then Sister Rachel's words sink in. "That little prick-"

Jay starts coughing loudly and Father McMann claps him hard on the back.

"You alright there, son?"

"Thank you, Father. Wrong pipe. You were saying, Mother?"

He gives me a pointed look.

"I was just saying what a little prickly eater our guest is. I'll have a talk with him, though. This is a House of God, not a free diner," I say sternly, and all the sisters smile fondly at me.

I notice Mark, Jay, Luke, and Matt staring at me, a proud grin on each of their faces, and I blush.

"Mother," Sister Mary-Francis calls, turning my attention, "I want to thank you again, so much, for speaking with the Bishop about my classes. They are going so well. I just can't believe you got him to reconsider."

The proud smirks on the Gospel Brothers' faces melt into frowns.

"What did Mother Evangeline do?" Mark wonders while giving me a censorious look.

"She got ol' Cunningham to give our girl, Mary-Francis, the money to get her master's degree!" Father McMann crows in delight.

I try not to wince at the accusatory look Mark shoots my way.

I fail when Father continues about how beneficial my "connection with the diocese" is.

Matt, Jay, and Luke are just shaking their heads, but I swear there's a ghost of amusement in Jay's eyes. I wonder how much trouble I'm going to be in when these four get me alone again.

Maybe they'll spank me this time.

"This is really nice," Sister Bernadette speaks, cutting off my naughty thoughts of punishment. "I wish we could do this more often."

I realize she's referring to eating dinner together.

The sisters always eat breakfast and lunch together, but our nights are simply too chaotic to try to form a habit of it. Poor Sister Rachel has to plan meals that can be made quickly, eaten on the go, and easily reheated for later.

But she never complains.

None of them do.

Nuns don't complain, bless them.

I try not to, too, but I mostly keep my mouth shut just in case I come across like an ungrateful sacrilege.

"Maybe tomorrow night," I offer to Sister Bernadette.

"Tomorrow's Thursday, remember?" Matt suddenly throws out.

I look at him blankly.

"Ah, no, I didn't. Thank you for the reminder," I say in confusion.

"We have the Diocesan Summit tomorrow and you said that you would join us; especially since you *know* Bishop Cunningham so well," Mark fills in.

Father McMann slaps his knee.

"I don't envy you boys having to drive up to Los Angeles for this. Perks of being retired, I guess. I didn't know that you were going, Mother Evangeline."

"Um, it was a last minute decision. I was under the weather this morning and it slipped my mind. Perhaps it would be best if I stayed behind," I offer.

"Oh, no, no, no. The sisters and I can run this place for a day, right, ladies?"

All the other nuns agree.

"Excellent," Mark says enthusiastically. "We'll be staying overnight, but we'll be back early Friday morning, in time for Lauds."

I feel my eyes bug out of my head.

I would be staying overnight somewhere with these forbidden sex-on-a-stick priests?!

Bad idea.

Baaaaaaaaaaaaaad idea.

We finish dinner and evening prayers, then everyone lumbers off to bed.

I glare at the Gospel Brothers, but leave to go check on Denny.

Jay snags my arm when I try to walk by him.

"Meet us down here when you're done," is all he says, but I swear his words are velvety with invitation.

I somehow manage to make it to the first floor without my pussy leaving a wet trail behind me, like some kind of holy snail slut. I get to Denny's door and bang loudly.

"Oy! I'm coming!" he calls out, taking his sweet-ass time to open up. "Oh hey, mommy, come on in."

"Goddammit, Denny! I told you it's 'mother', not fucking mommy. And what the hell is your problem? You couldn't eat the mushroom soup?"

"No! That shit was gross. I don't want no nasty ass mushrooms; unless they were shrooms, ya know what I mean? Ah fuck, were they shrooms and I missed out? Damn, everyone alw-"

My swift smack upside his head shuts him up.

"Are you seriously asking if *nuns* were eating psychedelic mushrooms in their motherfucking soup?"

"Well, when you put it that way. . . and you don't need to hit me. Sheesh, aren't you supposed to be godlier or some shit now that you can't have sex? And what were you thinking, anyway?! What a waste of a fine ass pussy- OUCH! Stop hitting me, woman!"

"Then shut up!" I counter. "Now listen, I'm going to be gone all day tomorrow and tomorrow night. I have a conference with the bishop."

"The who?"

"Haven't a clue. Some guy named the bishop; I don't know. I'll figure it out tomorrow. You are not to leave this convent under any circumstances. Not-"

"I know."

"Not for cigarettes, not for ass, not for-"

"RAE! I know," he reassures me.

"Ok, good. Oh, and I don't care if they make you crap on one of them Christ crackers, you're going to fucking eat it and like it. Got that?"

I give him my mean mother-look all nuns have.

He cowers a smidge.

"Yes, mommy."

I reach out and whap him again before leaving.

Outside his room, everything is silent.

The sisters have all gone to bed and Father McMann is back at the rectory.

I take a deep breath and head downstairs.

The lights are dimmed, but I can make out Jay, Matt, Luke, and Mark seated at the same table we ate dinner at. I walk over and try to corral my burgeoning passion. I recite the Ten Commandments, but get stuck on 'Thou Shalt Not Covet Thy Neighbor's Goods'.

I covet my current neighbors' goods, all right.

"What are you concentrating on so hard?" Matt wonders.

"Not coveting your dicks," I inadvertently reply.

I slap a hand over my mouth in horror, but the brothers don't look offended.

More strained and a little amused.

140

"That's what we want to talk to you about," Mark starts.

"Your dicks? You want to talk about your *priestly peckers?* Your brotherly boners? Your-"

Jay laughs outrightly, but the other smother their grins.

"No," Mark counters, "not specifically our penises, but about what happened here last night."

I pout.

I specifically want to talk about their consecrated cocks. . .

I suddenly realize that Mark is still talking.

"Yesterday was a mistake and we must endeavor to make sure that never happens again."

"Right," I agree while shaking me head in the negative.

"We're making a pact," Mark forges on. "We agree to not act on our obvious sexual urges. This is simply a test given to us by our Lord, and we must rise to the challenge."

"Don't say 'rise', it makes me think of your cocks," I blurt out.

Mark palms his face in his hand.

"Tomorrow's going to be a long day, isn't it?"

The others just grumble in agreement.

Chapter 15

The Gospel Truth

The next morning, we depart the convent early and drive the two hours to Los Angeles. We're in a black, fully-loaded Denali, and I have the backseat bench to myself. Mark is driving; Matt is in the passenger seat; Luke is behind Matt and Jay is next to him, in front of me.

I look around as I get comfy.

"I thought priests are supposed to be poor and shit," I comment.

"They are. They take a vow of poverty, but firstly, we're not priests just quite yet, and secondly, this was a gift from my family. It's large and can hold a lot of people and is great for carpooling and road trips," Mark answers.

"So, your family is rich?" I ask tactlessly.

"Loaded," Jay confirms, waggling his eyebrows.

Mark scoffs.

"You're one to talk. You family comes from old money."

Jay shrugs.

"And they still haven't learned that it can't buy you happiness."

His voice is laced with bitterness.

"I take it you don't approve?" I say.

"Quite the opposite, actually. *They* don't *approve* of *me*. Or rather, my decision to be a priest."

I frown.

"Well, that's a load of crap. You want to do something ethical and fulfilling with your life and they can't get behind that? Screw them," I sneer and I see Mark catch my eye in the rear-view mirror, a smirk on his face.

I guess that I'm not the only one who thinks Jay's family can go fuck themselves.

"You talk funny," Matt suddenly interjects.

"I do?"

"Yeah, you swear like a sailor and use a lot of slang, but at the same time, you're actually really well-spoken and articulate. It's. . . baffling."

I laugh at his confusion.

"Well, in my world, every other word is 'fuck', peppered with eight more swears words and who knows what else, so it kind of grows on you. I have to speak like this to fit in, but I'm not uneducated. Although, that's probably not why I speak so well. I like to read, so I have a large vocabulary. When I was a kid, it was my only escape sometimes."

"Were all the places you stayed at bad?" Luke asks.

"No. A couple of them were good homes and I miss those families, but most were neglectful. They weren't there to raise a child but to collect a check from the state. And some were downright awful. Abusive. No place for a child. There should be a better screening process for foster children. It's too easy to get forgotten and used."

I try not to sound rancorous, but I am.

I'm bitter to my very core about what happened in my youth.

"Evangeline," Mark starts, but I cut him off.

"My name's Raelynn, but I prefer Evangeline. It's prettier."

"Raelynn is pretty, too," Mark compliments softly, "but if you prefer Evangeline, we will call you that."

I nod, and he continues.

"I was just going to say I'm sorry and that you're right. Better care should be taken and more effort should be given where foster children are concerned. I hate that you had to experience neglect, let alone *abuse*."

His tone goes cold at the word, but I just shrug it off.

"It's no big deal. I'm over it."

Mark looks at me sharply in the mirror.

"What did I say about lying, Evangeline?" he reprimands sternly.

"Um, that you would bend me over your knee and spank me until I came if I kept doing it?" I joke.

Mark splutters an incoherent response, while Matt and Luke cough, but Jay. . .

Jay just grins.

We spend the rest of the trip in silence, but at least Mark stops asking me questions. Of course, now those years are all that I can think about. I try to focus on the few happy memories I have, but the poisonous ones keep overtaking my brain.

Namely, those years with my last foster family, before I ran away.

When I was nine, I was transferred to a new home. At the one before, my foster mom grew jealous of my looks and asked the state to find somewhere else for me. That's right, a thirty-something-year-old woman was jealous of a nine year old.

She said it right to my face and, to the social worker's disgust, to her face.

Penny, my social worker at the time, was a super sweet woman. In fact, she reminds me of my sisters back at the convent. Penny promised that she would look out for me and get me into the best home. I stayed with her for a couple of weeks while everything was finalized, but those fourteen days will live forever in my mind.

Penny took me shopping, to the movie theater, and even out to eat.

I begged Penny to keep me, but she said that she couldn't.

She swore giving me to a new foster family broke her heart, but not as much as it broke mine.

I know Penny pulled a lot of strings to get me into a special home.

A wholesome home.

A nonjudgmental home.

And on paper, the Hunt family looked perfect.

They were church-going and family oriented with their four kids, and graciously welcomed a fifth, me.

The first month in a new home is always the adaptation period. The time where you learn about the family behind the façade and if they wear a mask or are truly as they portray themselves.

For the most part, the Hunts were as they seemed. As one of them now, I was the oldest by many years, and my foster mom expected me to help out. Looking back, I sometimes wonder if their desire for an older foster child was simply to have an extra set of hands on call.

A free nanny of sorts.

I didn't mind though.

I've always loved kids, and the Hunt children were the cutest little things.

In my second month of living there, I got my period for the first time.

My foster mom was outraged and rushed me to the doctor, demanding to know 'my true age'. She was convinced the state was lying to her about how old I was. The doctor, bless him, asked her if she wanted him to cut me open and count the rings, and that I wasn't a damn tree. There was no way for him to 'know' my true age, other than what she was told.

He went on to explain that children my age can begin puberty, but my foster mom refused to listen.

In her mind, it wasn't normal.

It was the work of the Devil.

And that's when I learned a terrible truth: the more religious you are, the more fanatical you are in your beliefs. You feel like you have a personal mission on this Earth: to get everyone to believe in *your* dogma.

Instead of making my foster family more caring, loving, accepting, etc., their faith did the exact opposite.

It made them more disparaging and unsympathetic.

My foster mother took it upon herself to rid me of the demons that had 'possessed' me.

It's awkward to have boobs at nine.

It's even more awkward to have someone *tape* them down.

I already hated my body; I didn't need another reason to dislike it.

This went on for a year, until another social worker came in to check on me. I told her what my foster mom was doing, and she immediately intervened, but I wasn't removed from the house.

At that point, my foster mom was in a righteous fury.

She seemed hellbent to prove that her way of dealing with my body was the best way.

She started to dress me in tighter clothing.

Indecent, almost.

At ten, I had the body of a teenager, and it didn't help that I had a face to match.

Even before this, I drew the eyes of men, but now? They swarmed. My foster mother sat back, satisfied that she had proven her point while I was left to defend myself at every turn. I learned to never be alone. To always be with her or one of the younger children.

It worked, except there is one man that I couldn't escape.

One man who could corner me.

Punish me.

Control me.

My foster father.

He took my innocence and my hope, and I let him.

For three long years, I let him, but somehow, like with Walker, I got the gumption to say enough is enough.

And I had fucking enough.

I confessed everything to my foster mother, and she laughed at me outrightly. At first, I thought it was because she didn't believe me, but no. She did. But she knew no one else would. Her husband was one of the most well-regarded members of their church. A model citizen.

I was just a lying kid.

A troublesome kid, if she had a say in it.

Who would believe a bratty punk like me over her devout spouse?

I'll never forget my rage.

151

The unholy fury that still takes my breath away.

This woman wasn't fit to be a parent.

Hell, she wasn't fit to be anything. She was a disgrace, but she was right.

It was my word against theirs.

And I would lose.

Every.

Single.

Time.

So I said, 'fuck it', and I ran.

That year on my own was the coldest, hungriest, darkest year of my life.

But it was also my freest.

Chapter 16

Team Spirit, Bitches

"We're here."

Mark's words penetrate my brain and bring me back to the present.

I'm not quite sure where 'here' is, but it seems to be a really nice house in an extremely nice neighborhood.

"It's one of my parents' vacation rental houses. It's how they make their money. They have twenty and make more than a decent living off of it, but I told them about the summit awhile ago, and they reserved it for us to use. Come on inside and we can all stretch our legs."

I follow him inside the giant home, in awe.

It's the biggest house that I've ever been in.

People vacation in this place?

I swear that I'm not jealous as fuck or anything.

Hell, I've never even been on a vacation before.

Unless we're counting this little road trip, which would be sad, right?

Mark shows me to a spacious room, and I thank him.

I place Sister Evangeline's suitcase on the bed. I don't really know why I brought it. All I have is another habit to change into. I'm in my room for ten minutes or so, before Luke taps on my open door.

"Change of plans," he says, his serious face unsmiling.

His eyes are such a piercing blue under the fringe of his dark lashes and hair, I swear that I could lose myself under their hypnotic gaze.

"The summit was cancelled. Bishop Cunningham had a stroke."

His words bring me up short and I gasp.

"Is he alright?" I ask in genuine concern, even though I've never even met the man.

"Yes, he's stable."

"Thank God."

Luke gives me a small smile.

"Yes, thank the Lord."

I roll my eyes at him.

154

"So, what now? Are we just going to drive back?"

I really didn't want to get back into the car so soon.

"Um, no, actually. We thought. . ."

Luke trails off as if he's embarrassed.

"You thought what?" I prompt when he doesn't continue.

"We thought maybe we would stay and go out. Not like on a date," he rushes to explain. "But just to give you a break from. . .pretending."

I'm taken aback at his words.

They want to give me a break?

And do something fun?

Who are these men and can I keep them?

"Yeah, ok, that sounds fun."

"Great, Jay will be right back with some clothes. Meet us downstairs when you're changed."

Luke leaves and Jay comes in a bit later, holding some articles of clothing. He's wearing jeans and t-shirt and looks. . . scrumptious.

I scowl.

155

"Where are your priest clothes?" I demand.

He laughs at my outrage.

"Priests can wear layman's clothes, too, you know. And I'm not a priest yet. Get changed and get back downstairs. We're all hungry and want to go eat."

Food?

I can get behind that.

I look at the simple black leggings and white tank top and tears prick my eyes.

It's been a long time since someone has just given me something, no strings attached.

Walker gave me plenty of gifts, but they came with a really high price tag.

I change and slip back on the sandals that I've been nunning in.

It feels so good to be in normal clothes.

I'm not much of a dress-person and a habit is more like a freaking muumuu anyway.

I shake my long hair out and let it hang around me like a cape, the riotous curls weaving around my arms. I take a glance in the mirror, pleased, and then turn to go meet the guys, but something glittery and gold catches my eye.

I bounce back and assess my reflection.

My shirt says, 'Team Spirit', and has a dove flying through the words.

Those smartasses.

I bound downstairs to confront them.

"A Jesus shirt, really?"

"What, I think it's hilarious," Matt says. "Team Spirit for the Holy Spirit, get it?"

"I get it," I tell him, rolling my eyes.

"Well, don't blame me," he laughs. "Jay's the one who got it."

I turn to glare at Jay, but he's looking at me critically.

"What's wrong?" I wonder.

"It didn't show that much skin on the mannequin," he finally announces, disgruntled.

"Um, well, that's probably because mannequins don't have skin," I return jokingly.

Now, he rolls his eyes.

157

"What do you want to do today?" Mark asks me.

I chew on my lower lip.

"I don't know. . . I really have never gotten out much."

"What do you mean?" Luke says.

"I never really ever left the complex unless Walker needed me to. It was safer in my room. Actually, his room, but whatever."

"You've basically been a prisoner for nineteen years?" Jay questions in shock.

"I mean, I chose to stay inside. No one forced me," I try to explain.

"Walker never took you out?"

"Like on a date?" I snort. "Of course not. I've actually never been on a date."

I wonder if I look pathetic at my confession.

"Me, neither," Luke says quietly next to me, and I instantly feel better.

"Well, this isn't a date," Mark inserts firmly.

"Yes, *father*," I tease.

He reaches out to swat me playfully and I laugh.

"What? I'm just calling you by your proper title! Like Father McMann. It's not like I called you *daddy*."

All four men groan at my words.

"Remember the pact?" Matt reminds.

"Nope," I tease because it's just too easy.

"Promise that you'll behave today," Mark instructs and I scowl at him.

"I always behave!" I protest.

"Were you behaving the other night when we found you. . ." Luke trails off dryly.

"When you caught me getting off?"

More groaning.

"This is what Mark means when he asked if you are going to behave yourself," Matt points out.

"Am I supposed to be ashamed of my sexuality? Why did God make me a sexual creature if I'm not supposed to own it? And besides, it's not *my* fault that I was so horny. It was your guys'!"

"Our fault!" Matt exclaims, his hazel eyes wide in disbelief. "What did we do?!"

159

"Oh, please. Look at yourselves. Now throw in some basketball, which really is just passive-aggressive foreplay, and there you go."

"Passive-aggressive foreplay?" Jay smirks.

Of course, Mark steps up in his leader role.

"We're sorry. It was never our intention to. . ."

"Turn me on?"

Mark sighs.

"Yes, we didn't mean to 'turn you on'. As for your questions: I don't think God wants you to shun your sexuality, but to treat it with respect. Your body is a temple and only one true worshipper should be allowed. And that's your husband," he clarifies.

"My body, my temple, right? And if it's a temple, doesn't that make me the Goddess? If so, then why the hell would I settle for just *one* worshipper? I want them *all*. And I don't want to them to treat my temple with respect, I want them to fucking defile it until I can't move."

The Gospel Brothers all take a ragged breath and make the sign of the cross.

This is going to be one interesting non-date.

Chapter 17

Stop, In the Name of God

The guys surprise me and take me to an adult arcade after we eat.

I've never had such fun. They teach me to play all the games. I really like Skee-ball and air hockey. Skee-ball is Mark's favorite. We each take turns asking one another questions as we roll the balls.

"What your favorite color?"

Toss.

"Burgundy. When did you decide to become a priest?"

Toss.

"At nineteen. Did you ever want to be something growing up?"

Toss.

"A mermaid. What's your favorite number?"

"Six-six-six."

His answer catches me off guard and I lob the ball sideways and off my ramp into another player's lane. Mark and I dissolve into a fit of laughter as I try to apologize. The guy just shrugs.

"At least you got in the seventy-five thousand hole," he remarks, handing me one of his balls.

I toss my last ball as Jay, Matt, and Luke come over.

"How many tickets do you have?" Jay asks.

He's five times more competitive than Mark.

And Mark is pretty freaking competitive for a priest-to-be.

"I don't know, like two-hundred and two," I offer.

"Cool. I've got like seven-hundred and twelve, but who's counting?"

I smirk at the obnoxious man.

"Who's up for a game of laser tag?" Matt asks.

"What does the winner get?" Jay demands.

Matt makes a face.

"I thought we could just play-"

"Really?" I tease. "You thought Jay and Mark could just 'play'?"

"Good point. Ok, what are the stakes?"

"I say the winner gets to choose what we do tonight," I propose. "So, if I win and I decide that we all must watch *The Black Cauldron*, everyone has to."

"*The Black Cauldron?*" Luke wonders.

"Yes. I still have no idea what Gurgi is, besides a little scamp."

Jay just shakes his head at me.

"Sure, we can watch some antiquated Disney movie if you win, but you won't. So, basically resign yourself to whatever *I* decide."

"Challenge. Accepted," I growl.

We buy our game passes and get geared up. The arena is large enough that each of us can play individually and have a 'home' to guard. I'm going to infiltrate these pious pricks' safe zone and we're going to watch the Horned King reap souls. That creepy bastard still gives me nightmares.

The person working comes around to check our gear and to remind us of the rules, which are little. This is

163

basically a free-for-all. I look at the guys. Mark's color is red; Jay's is yellow, Matt's is green, and Luke's is blue. And I'm rocking purple.

We are each given a map with just the location of our 'home base'. Really, without teams, it's a coin toss of whether to guard your 'home' or try to take down another person's. The place is large and when I locate my base, it's somewhat hidden. It might be worth going after the others'.

I cringe when I take in my white shirt.

It glows brightly in the blacklights.

This won't do.

I still have sixty seconds before our guns power up, so I wiggle out of the shirt and tuck it inside my vest, which covers everything. You really couldn't see the shirt, except at the bottom, where it's longer than the vest, but it still will call attention.

So off it goes.

This is war, and a Disney movie is at stake.

The music amps up as our guns engage, our signal to begin the game.

I have fifteen minutes to kick ass.

164

I let my dark hair swing around me like a cape of darkness, blocking my vest's lights and target centers.

Is this cheating?

Probably.

Do I care?

Nope.

Stealthily, I crouch into a crawl and start moving around.

I can see the map in my head and I set out to raise hell.

The first color that I encounter is blue.

Luke.

Before he knows what's happening, I shoot him and run.

I round a corner and slam into someone lit up with red.

Mark.

"Ouch!" I cry, and instantly Mark lowers his gun in concern.

"Are you alr-"

I reach up and shoot him in the heart center.

"I'm fine, thanks."

Then, I dash off.

I search and search for yellow and green, but I don't find Jay and Matt.

Somewhere in the arena, I hear angry shouting. The other guys must have met up with one another. I weave around two more corners and make my way to the upper level. A flash of light catches my eye, and I get down low, making sure to cover the lights on my gun.

I peep around a corner and see yellow lights blinking.

Jay.

He has his back turned and is looking at something.

His home!

I smile evilly as I shoot him in the back, disarming him.

He lets out a surprised yelp and whirls around, still not seeing me.

Just as his lights activate again, I shoot him once again.

I do this four times before he finally steps away from his base. Of course, his large body still blocks my target. I need to get closer. I stand up, allowing my purple lights to show. I hear his gasp and chuckle. Just as he charges back up, I beam my laser at him, one more rendering him gunless.

"Wanna go get the others together?" I tempt.

"No," he says sourly.

Someone's a sore loser.

I spend another few minutes toying with him, deciding how to get him to move, when an idea strikes me. I shoot him again and he growls in anger at his dilemma. Making sure my hair cover my back targets, I sidle up to Jay. He looks at me warily, tossing a look behind him. He's making it very obvious that he's guarding something.

"What's behind you, Jay?" I purr, looking into his bright blue eyes.

His hair is so fair, it practically glows in the black lights.

"Nothing," he lies.

I feel my brows raise.

"Did you just *lie?* Tsk-tsk, someone is a naughty boy."

He glares at me, but I keep walking until I'm in his personal space. His soft gasp says that I've rattled him. I hear his gun charge back up, but I'm not concerned. I've got him cornered. Without breaking eye-contact, I reach up on my tiptoes and kiss his full mouth. His eyes widen and fill with something akin to panic.

"Evangeline, don-"

I let go of my gun and cup his face, kissing him fiercely, no longer playing the game.

To my surprise, it's Jay's tongue that comes out to caress my lips. I open my mouth, beckoning him in and then we fall off the precipice into a sea of lust. His hands stroke up and down my bare arms and I pull his head down so that I can kiss him deeper.

My feverish whimpers bring me back to the present, and I break the kiss.

Jay stares down at me, his eyes unreadable.

He leans down to kiss me again, this time pulling back when he's done.

"I'm going to Hell for this, but it was worth the taste," he whispers and tears prick my eyes.

"You're not going to Hell, Jay. You're a good man. If anyone is going to Hell, it's me," I admit ruefully.

"No, you're not. You're a good person, too. A sweet person whose been dealt a bad hand. You're just trying to make the best of it you can."

I smile at him.

He really is too sweet for his own.

I kiss his cheek chastely.

"Thank you for that," I tell him. "And thank you for this."

"What?" he asks in confusion.

"The winning shot."

Then, I raise my gun behind him and shoot around until the sound of a fake explosion goes off.

I just shot his 'home base'.

The music ends, signaling that our fifteen minutes are up.

Jay groans.

"You wicked little vixen. If you had wanted to watch that movie so badly, we would have," Jay chastises.

I grin broadly.

"Nope, I changed my mind. I have something else that I want to play."

Chapter 18

Never Have I Ever

"I can't believe that she shot your base!" Mark grumbles. "How did that even happen? I figured we would smoke her-"

"Hey!" I yell in indignation from the far back of the Denali. "You're just jealous that I creamed you all!"

"I really don't want to watch The Black Cauldron," Mark whines and I laugh.

"We're not, you big baby. But we need to stop and get some wine."

I see Mark's eyebrows raise in the rearview mirror.

"Wine? For what?"

"We're going to play 'Never Have I Ever'," I announce triumphantly.

Mark frowns at me, and then chuckles.

"What's so funny?" I demand.

171

"Fine, my phony sister. We can play your game, but I have a feeling you're even more sheltered than we are," he teases and I scowl.

"I'm not sheltered," I argue, but Mark only smirks at me.

I'll show him who's sheltered.

"Does that mean you're going to play?" I challenge.

"You bet. My parents have good wine at the house; we can open a bottle, but I doubt much gets drank."

I narrow my eyes at his ill-concealed taunt.

Bring.

It.

On.

We get to the house and the guys go off to change into sweats. It still unnerves me to see them dressed like this. It makes me forget that they're becoming priests. Everyone gets comfy in the living room. Jay turns on the TV and turns on a show to have in the background. He still hasn't spoken a word to me since the game, but when our eyes meet, there's a fiery passion burning in his.

Mark comes back with five wine goblets and a bottle of dark wine.

"Are priests allowed to drink?"

He gives me a funny look.

"Of course. There's nothing wrong with alcohol. It only becomes a problem when someone indulges in it too much and too often, but God didn't bring us here to be miserable. He wants us to be happy and to enjoy ourselves."

"Then why can't you have sex?"

"Because God specifically dictated that sex is only meant for the confines of marriage."

I mull over this while we all get situated.

"Maybe God didn't mean for marriage to be interpreted in just one way. Kind of like how you don't think love is only meant for a man and a woman," I ponder.

Mark looks at me, his curly brown hair creating an unruly halo around his upper face. He studies me intently, quizzically almost, before responding with a simple 'maybe'.

"Evangeline, this is your game. You start," Matt directs, as Mark pours us each half a glass of wine.

"Um, okay. Never have I ever kissed a boy."

I'm the only one to take a drink.

"Jay, your turn," I tell him.

"Never have I ever been married."

No one takes a drink.

"My turn," Matt announces. "Never have I ever kissed a girl."

Mark and Jay each take a drink.

I gasp.

"You've kissed a woman?!"

"You," Jay remarks dryly.

"Just me?" I demand.

He looks away for a moment.

"No. I was engaged for a long time."

I can hear the ache in his voice and my heart stutters at the sound.

"Were you engaged, too?" I ask Mark.

"No, but I was young once," he jokes.

I roll my eyes.

"You're still young," I mumble. "Your turn, Luke."

"Never have I ever taken the Lord's name in vain."

"Wait, like swore?"

"Yes, but using the word 'God' with it."

"Oh."

Big gulp for me on this one.

Surprisingly, all the others drink, too.

"Sinners!" I yell, pointing at them, and we all laugh.

"Ok, my turn again. Never have I ever gotten myself off."

All four of my guys take a drink. I don't bother.

"Never have I ever gotten myself off recently," I throw out.

"Woah there, it's not even your turn," Mark points out, but Jay interrupts him.

"What's recently?"

"The last week," I stipulate.

"Well, I'm good then," Jay smirks, "but you better drink up."

I glower at him.

"You, too, pal! You got off this week!"

175

"Yeah, but it wasn't me who did it," he corrects.

Oh.

Damn.

He's right.

That one's all on me.

Jay laughs and winks at my face.

"You should probably drink twice for that one," he mocks.

I stick my tongue out at him but from the corner of my eye, I see Matt discreetly raise his glass to his mouth and take a sip.

"Matt was jacking off!" I publicize gleefully and he blushes bright red.

He looks down, appearing forlorn, and I feel like a jerk.

"Hey, Mattie, I was just teasing. There's nothing wrong with a little self-love. . ."

Is there?

Catholics have rules for everything. Maybe masturbation *is* wrong.

I furrow my brow, thinking out loud, "Is it bad to touch yourself?"

"Yes. No. There's a lot of gray area there. Matt, you didn't do anything wrong," Mark soothes.

"Yes, I did, and you know it," he mumbles.

"No, you didn't. We're becoming priests, not God. We're not trying to be perfect; we're just trying to be better. Sometimes, we might stumble, but that doesn't mean all is lost," Mark coaches.

Matt raises his head and locks eyes with Mark.

"And you'll always be there to guide me back?"

"Always, brother. Always."

I ruin the moment when I fan my eyes that are welling up with tears and yell, "AWWWWWWW!"

All four men chuckle.

"I think that's enough of this game," Mark decrees.

"You're right. We should drink the rest of the wine and play spin the bottle," I proclaim.

Luke chokes on his swallow of fermented grape juice that he was sipping.

"Kidding, I was kidding, sheesh. Although, if anyone needs to play that game, it's you two," I tell Luke and Matt.

"Why us?"

"Because you've never kissed a woman! That's like a rite of passage. You can't become a priest without lip-locking at least once in your life."

"What kind of logic is that?" Mark wonders.

"Fake nun logic, boys."

I drain the rest of my glass and pour myself another.

A real one.

Not any of this 'half a glass' shit.

Since we're not playing anymore, I down it in three swallows.

This shit, whatever it is, tastes way better than the Lord's blood.

No offense, Jesus.

"I think we should all get some rest. We have to be up pretty early to drive back to San Bernardino."

"Ok," I acquiesce, "but first everyone is getting a good-night kiss from me."

Chapter 19

Deadly Sinning

I realize that I'm a little tipsy, but I'm giving Matt and Luke their rite of passage, dammit.

I saunter over to Matt, and no one tries to stop me. It's like they're frozen in their seats. Even sitting down, Matt is barely shorter than me. I lean down infinitesimally, my hair creating a curtain between us and the rest of the world.

I lick my lips nervously when I see the hesitation in Matt's gorgeous hazel eyes.

"Can I kiss you? Please?"

"Evangeline, we shouldn't-"

"*Please*," I beg in a husky whisper and he groans.

"One kiss. Just one-"

I seal my lips over his before he can change his mind.

Holy fuck.

For someone who says that they've never kissed another person, kudos to this guy. Maybe he's been practicing on himself. Remember in junior high, when everyone would make out with their hand? Maybe he never stopped doing it and it's paying off for us both now.

Matt moans underneath me and I take that as an invitation to plop myself in his lap.

I mean, if this is going to be his only kiss, we probably shouldn't half-ass it.

I throw myself into our kiss, body and soul.

Also with some dry humping.

Matt's arms squeeze around me like a vice and I can feel myself tumbling headfirst into something unknown.

Someone snags me from behind and pulls me off Matt; we both protest. Of course, it's Mark, the brother of reason and single temple-worshipping logic.

"You're a dangerous woman, Evangeline," Mark says darkly.

"What's that supposed to mean?"

"Exactly as it implies. You don't wave a buffet in front of a starving man."

"Are you *starving?*" I inquire curiously.

"*Fucking ravenous,*" Jay answers for Mark, startling us both with his words.

The bright blue of his eyes is shadowed by his pupils, blown wide with desire. His hand rests next to his rock-hard dick, which is straining against his sleep pants. He makes no move to touch it, but he doesn't hide it either.

Everyone is staring at Jay like he's grown two heads; I guess he sort of did. For some reason, I look over at Luke, and I almost fall over. He's staring at Jay with an unfathomable yearning. He sees me looking at him and quickly averts his eyes from Jay's raging boner, but it's too late.

I've seen something he's never wanted anyone to see.

"Luke's turn," I say lightly.

I walk over to the gorgeously tall man, pushing a dark lock of his hair out of his eyes. Their hue is even more piercing than Jay's.

"That is, if you want one," I add, unsure after what I'd just seen.

Luke captures my wrist lightly, tugging me forward.

181

"I want one more than you know," he rasps, and the same hunger that he had looked at Jay with, he now turns on me.

I slip a knee alongside his left thigh, wedging myself between him and the recliner. Again, I use my long dark hair to create a divide between us and the outside world. Our eyes never close as I lean in and rub my nose sweetly along his, then I turn my head to whisper in his ear.

"I accept you. You have nothing to hide from me, but your secret is safe. I will never tell anyone, but please know that you have nothing to be ashamed of. Who you love is who you love. And I fucking *love* the thought of you and Jay together."

I bring myself down into his lap as I finish my announcement and Luke's dick literally convulses underneath me at my words.

When I pull back, there are tears in his eyes; although, it might just be a trick of the light.

I kiss him then and it's exactly as I thought it would be, sweetly innocent.

I don't try to deepen the kiss, but merely let his lips explore mine.

182

When he sighs, I tentatively run my tongue between our mouths, and then I pull back.

Poor Luke looks stunned.

This time, I'm the one to move, of my own accord, and I ease off Luke gently.

"Bedtime," Mark announces grimly.

"I'll clean up down here," I volunteer.

I'm not quite ready for sleep; I'm too wired.

Mark nods at me and waits to follow the others upstairs, making sure they are all in their rooms. What a little mother hen, but I think it's cute how he's worried about their virtue. I chuckle at this. It's no use telling Mark that I don't plan to corrupt his brothers any more than I have.

I carry the glasses to the kitchen, clean them, and put them away. There's only a quarter left of the bottle of wine, so I figure that I'll drink it.

Waste not, want not, right?

"Do you need some help finishing that?" a voice calls behind me.

Jay.

And he's still wearing that look.

The sexy-as-fuck one that says he's ready to denounce his vows and sell his soul to the fucking Devil if it means he can have a go at me.

I can't honestly say that I'm not down for that either.

"Sure," I concede, offering him a swig only after I take a healthy one myself. "Does Daddy Mark know that you're down here? I mean Brother Mark. I guess he's not a father yet."

Jay carefully takes the bottle from me to have his own drink.

"Why? Do you want him to join us?" he asks and I feel everything inside of me tighten with need at his words.

"You're bad," I breathe.

"Not yet, but I think I'm going to be very soon," he admits.

He takes one more swig from the bottle and sets in on the kitchen counter, before placing a hand on either side of me. My butt is pressed against the cabinets and my legs feel wobbly already.

"W-w-what do you mean?" I stammer.

184

"Why tell you when I can show you?" he asks, pressing his chest to mine.

My eyes feel larger than saucers at his boldness.

This isn't some meek and unsure priest; this is a man.

A man who clearly knows what he wants.

And he wants me.

He leans even further into my personal space, breathing in my perfumed hair. I watch the curls dance and tickle around his nose.

"You're gorgeous, Evangeline," he whispers. "You're so pure, so good, even though you don't think so. I see it and I know it. And I want to taste that goodness."

Then he dips his mouth to mine and claims me.

All the passion is there from before, but now it's raw.

Unchecked.

His hands scoop me under my ass and lift until I am seated at the edge of the kitchen counter, my core perfectly aligned with his rock-hard cock. I claw at his shirt, tugging it over and off his body, so that I can run my hands over his muscled front and back.

I love the feel of him as he tenses under my exploratory touch.

Our mouths never part as I hook my thumbs into the waistband of his sweats and tug them down. His straining cock pops free and I fist it hard, jerking the velvety smoothness up and down.

"Argh," he garbles. "Slow down, sweetheart, or else I'm going to embarrass myself."

"I thought you already did?" I tease, referring to the other night when he came in pants just from me dry humping him.

He growls low in his throat and nips at my bottom lip.

Before I can comprehend what's happening, he lifts me from the counter and walks me to the kitchen table, setting me down on top of it.

"Let's see who's embarrassed in a minute," he threatens darkly, pushing me back to lie down.

I prop myself up on my elbows to see what he's doing, but he glares at me, and I quickly lean back. I stare at the ceiling, wondering what he's up to, when I feel his hot breath against my pussy, through my thread-bare leggings.

I can feel him kissing and licking me through the material, working my clit, and it drives me insane.

Is this what wearing a condom feels like?

No wonder no one uses them.

This sucks.

"Here, let me take them off," I attempt, but he pushes me back.

"Don't move," he commands firmly and I swear more liquid gushes out of me at the tone of his voice.

He goes back to mouth-fucking me through the leggings.

This time, he adds his fingers, touching me lightly, teasingly.

I buck against his.

I can't help it.

"Please, please. . . *please*," I whine breathlessly.

"Please, what?"

"Please take off my pants."

"No, not until you embarrass yourself," he remarks darkly, pinching my clit hard to prove a point.

187

I scream as I come and Jay quickly claps a hand over my mouth, his eyes wide in shock.

"You came from *that?*" he asks incredulously.

I blush.

"I. . . I like it rough."

He groans.

"Of course you do," he teases.

"Have I been sufficiently embarrassed?"

He chuckles.

"Not even close, but I'm done fucking around."

His words surprise me, but his hands forcefully yanking off my pants stun me silent. He pulls them free; then he shucks his sweats to the side, his long dick finally unobstructed. I slip off the table and kneel before him.

"Jesus, Jay, you're huge," I say, taking the tip of his impressive length into my mouth.

I suckle for a moment before I take him fully into my mouth.

I stroke up and down only twice, before Jay fists my hair and pulls me up to him. Hitching my legs up, I wrap myself around him once more, aligning my center with him.

The tip of his cock pulses against my pussy and I look into his eyes as he slides into my wet core.

"Oh God, Evangeline. I'm not going to last," Jay confesses.

I entwine my arms around his neck, kissing him deeply before saying, "I've been dreaming of you filling my pussy up with your cum."

He snarls, walking over to the kitchen wall and pushing me against it roughly.

"I'm not coming in you. Fuck, I'm not even wearing a condom," he moans.

"My tubes are tied. A gift from Walker when I turned eighteen," I say bitterly.

His eyes catch mine at my words. He doesn't say anything, but he doesn't need to.

"Hold onto me, baby," he orders, still looking into my eyes.

And then he fucks me.

Hard.

My ass slams against the wall as his thighs slap against mine.

He feels so good inside of me.

Jay reaches down a hand to tickle my clit and like before, he pinches me hard.

The unexpected pain sends me over and I cry out loudly as I spasm around his cock.

He buries his face into my hair and gives a muffled shout as he follows me over the edge.

We stay like this for a while, trying to catch our breath.

"How the hell didn't we wake the whole house?" I wonder.

"It's a miracle of God," Jay teases and I laugh.

"Thank you," I whisper to him.

"Don't thank me yet, angel," he says cryptically.

Then he carries me upstairs and tucks me in bed, where I sleep.

Alone.

Chapter 20

Spiritual Guidance

Late morning sun streams through the window of the guest room. I look at the clock; it reads 10:45. So much for making it back in time for Lauds. I launch out of the comfy bed and quickly pull on my habit. I don't bother with my veil, instead, I throw all my belongings in the real Sister Evangeline's suitcase and head downstairs, afraid the guys left me.

Of course, I should have known better.

The Gospel Brothers are not douches.

They never would have left me behind.

I find Mark and Matt in the kitchen and all of last night's memories flood my mind.

Jay in front of me.

Jay behind me.

Jay in me.

"Ahh!" I cry, shaking my head.

Instantly, Mark is up and at my side.

"Evangeline! Are you alright?"

"No! I need you to perform an exorcism on my brain! I swear it's fucking possessed with-"

I abruptly stop talking.

"Possessed with what?" Mark barks out.

"Demons. My demons haunt me."

Mark frowns at me, but doesn't press for more.

"Where are Luke and Jay?" I ask, trying to keep my voice even when I speak my one-night stand's name.

"Luke is getting everything packed up into the SUV, and Jay. . ."

"Jay's left," Matt supplies curtly.

My heart starts to beat faster.

"Left?! Left for where?" I demand.

"To see the Archbishop," comes Mark's cryptic reply.

"Oh," I say in relief.

That doesn't sound bad.

"Well, are we going to wait for him or pick him up?"

The two men don't say anything and it's then that I note the worry in Mark's honeyed eyes and the tenseness in Matt's shoulders. Realization makes a sinking sensation deep in the pit of my stomach.

"He's not coming back with us, is he?" I whisper.

Both men shake their heads.

"Why-" I falter, afraid to ask. "Why did he go the Archbishop?"

No one says anything for a beat and then Mark heaves a heavy sigh.

"He's decided not to become a priest."

There's no judgement when his eyes meet mine, but I still feel the unspoken reproach.

"Did he say why?" I ask dully.

"No. I was hoping you could maybe tell us about this spur-of-moment decision."

I can't look Mark in the eyes; so I just shrug and mumble listlessly something about going to wait outside in the Denali.

I climb into the SUV; Luke sees me, but barely even acknowledges my existence.

Is this my fault?

Did I tear the Gospel Brothers apart?

Stupid question.

Of course, I did.

The ride back to San Bernardino is a sober and silent one.

I burn with a thousand doubts and regrets.

How much did the others know?

Did Jay tell them everything and Mark is just trying to get me to confess?

Father McMann is waiting for us when we arrive.

"Brothers, Mother. I'm glad to see you made it back safely. Mother Evangeline, the sisters have need of you.

Son," Father McMann says, turning Mark, "I got your message. Let's go talk."

They walk toward the rectory and I scurry into the convent like my lying-ass is on fire.

Inside, I find Sister Agatha.

"Oh, thank goodness, Mother! You've returned. Sister Bernadette is sick and her after-school catechism kids are here. Can you take over her class?"

"Of course," I bluff. "How long is the class?"

"An hour."

"No worries. You go see if Sister Bernadette needs anything and I will be downstairs teaching."

"Oh, thank you, Mother!"

I wave her off and walk to the basement to the CCD room. Maybe an hour of corralling small children while trying to teach them to be holy and shit will take my mind off of Jay. I open the door to go inside, but instead of finding children, I find a room full of about eleven teenagers.

"Ah. . ." I stutter before getting ahold of myself. "Good afternoon, everyone. I'm Mother Evangeline. I'll be taking over for Sister Bernadette, who is ill. Can someone help me out with what you've been doing in class?"

One particularly eager girl waves her hand.

"Yes, redhead in the front."

"Ginger," she corrects.

"Oh, sorry. I didn't think redheads liked to be called that. Ok, ginger in the front, go ahead."

"No, Mother. *My* name is *Ginger.*"

Oh, for the love of God. What the hell were her parents smoking?

"Right. Ginger. Fitting. What are we working on?"

"Sister Bernadette has been going through a 'Devotional for Teens' a week," she says, waving a pamphlet.

"Ok. Awesome. That's easy enough. And what is this week's topic?"

"*If God Loves Me, Why Can't I Own and Operate a Midget Brothel?*" Ginger reads.

"The fuck you say-" I sputter and everyone gasps.

Shit.

Damage control time.

"*The fuck you say* is probably what you're thinking, but the Lord has a plan and it doesn't include your foul mouths. Even your mental one. You must cleanse yourself of the habit of cursing," I say sternly and I few students nod.

I look around until I find an extra pamphlet. Sure as shit it reads just as Ginger announced.

What the hell am I supposed to say to this?!

"Alright. I think we'll do an open discussion about this week's topic. I'll start. The Lord and Baby Jesus don't want you to own and operate a midget brothel because that's profiling. And politically incorrect. Midgets don't like to be called this. I'm not sure what they want to be called, but if you're going to own and operate a brothel, you'll want some diversity. That's just smart business ethics there. That way you can cater to all your clients' needs. A lot of whores means more to choose from. Anyone want to take it from here?"

Ginger is waving her hand obnoxiously.

"Let's hear from someone else. You, boy in the back who looks like he would rather be anywhere but here, what's your take?"

"It's illegal to operate brothels," he points out.

"Not in most of Nevada."

Again, Ginger tries to get my attention.

I ignore her.

Another boy raises his hand and I call on him.

"This is a little off-topic, but is it a sin to whack off to your best friend's mom?"

"Absolutely not. Now, propositioning her is another matter. Actually, it's if she propositions you. Let's just be safe and say no banging your best friend's mom, but dumping your load to the image of her washing dishes? Totally fine. Anyone else?"

By this point, everyone has their hand in the air.

I'm fucking killing it at nunning today.

Mark might even be a little proud of me.

I'm about to call on another kid when someone knocks on the door.

"Come in," I call and in rushes Sister Mary-Francis.

Her face is pale and worried.

"Ok, that's all for today. You can all go and Sister Bernadette should be back to teaching you next week."

The class sounds with 'boos' and 'ahhs' as I follow Sister Mary-Francis out.

"They seem really taken with you, Mother; not that I'm surprised. You have that effect on people."

"Oh, why thank you, sister. Now, what's wrong? You look upset."

"It's Denny, Mother. He's gone."

Fuck.

I'd forgotten about Denny.

"And he left a note. It was on top of a pack of cigarettes."

She hands me a piece of paper with scratchy handwriting. It says 'They've found me and I won't let them get you or hurt your nun friends. Thanks for everything.'

Double fuck.

I need to find Mark and the other two ASAP.

Chapter 21

Herpes from Hell

I burst into the rectory without even knocking.

"Mother Evangeline, is everything ok?" Father McMann inquires, taking in my panicked look.

"No, I need to speak with the brothers immediately."

He nods and Mark, Luke, and Matt follow me back to the convent to Denny's room.

"He's gone," I say succinctly. "He left me some cigarettes and a note."

I show the guys what Denny wrote, chewing my lip in worry. When no one says anything, I start pacing.

"How did someone find him? What should I do? Should I run? Are my sisters in trouble?"

Luke looks thoughtful.

"Anyone could have tailed him. As for your other question, I don't think it would hurt to alert the authorities.

We have no idea who was after Denny, but I doubt you need to-"

"The Outcasts of Hell were after him," I confess and for a second time, I hear Mark swear.

"Son of a bitch! Why would you harbor someone who knows you, here *where you are?!*"

Tears well up in my eyes.

"I know! I'm sorry! It was stupid, but he needed help and I know that I've endangered the others-"

"I don't care about the others!" Mark roars and then calms down. "I mean, I do, but I'm concerned about you."

"Evangeline, you need to leave. You need to go to the police and get into a witness protection program," Matt says.

"No. I can't go to the police. Do you know how many dirty cops Walker has working on the inside? Plus, I have no intention of testifying against them; therefore, no witness protection program for me. And I can't run. I literally don't own a single I.D."

All three guys look contemplative as they try to think of ideas.

"I might be able to help," Mark finally says reluctantly. "Let me makes some calls. Hopefully, in a couple of days, I'll have some answers and a solution. In the meantime, there's no leaving the convent. And you must wear your veil at *all* times. Understand? Walker is dangerous, but he isn't going to just come in and shoot an unidentified nun."

I nod my understanding.

"Good. Ok, I'll reconvene with you later tonight."

He starts to walk away, and Luke and Matt follow.

"Oh, and Evangeline?" Mark calls.

"Yes?"

"No smoking!"

Later that night, I'm in my room.

For once, I'm actually praying.

*Dear God, it's me again. Mother Evangeline.
Actually, just Evangeline. Actually, really Raelynn.*

Dear God, I'm rambling in prayer.

I attempt to start over.

*Listen, I know you're a really super busy dude and all,
but my friend Denny needs your help. Please watch over his
dumbass. Also, please watch over my sisters. They are
good nuns and have nunthing to do with this. I hope that
nun pun made you laugh. Oh, and I forgot about Jay.
Please look out for him, too. I'm sorry I corrupted one of
your good ones; I promise not to touch the others. Amen.*

I nod toward Heaven.

God can't ignore my pleas when I make nun jokes,
right?

A light tapping on my door brings me out of my
musings. I pad over and open it to find Mark.

"Can I come in?"

"I don't know? Can you or will God strike you down
for entering a nun's room?" I tease.

He mock glares at me and slips in, shutting the door.

"Everything alright?"

"Not really. I've lost one of my best friends today and I'm doing something illegal."

I feel my eyes widen at his announcement.

"Let's start with the last part. What are you doing that's illegal?"

"I'm trying to get you some fake I.D.s," he confesses.

"Oh, Mark," I murmur, my heart in my throat. "Thank you!"

I reach over and hug him tightly.

"Now, what's this about losing a best friend?"

"Jay?" he says dryly.

"Well, I figured, but you make it seem like he's dead!"

Mark hangs his head.

"I was supposed to be there for him. He depended upon me to keep him on the straight and narrow. He wanted to be a priest so badly, I just can't understand why-"

"We had sex!" I blurt out, and then cringe.

Another sigh from Mark.

"I guessed, but since neither of you said anything before, I didn't want to make any assumptions."

"I'm sorry," I mumble.

Mark smiles at me ruefully.

"Don't apologize. Besides, it takes two to tango."

I chuckle at his words.

"I hate saying this, but I think you did Jay a favor," he admits.

"Really?"

"Yes. Jay is a family man. He wants a wife and children."

"Then why was he trying to be a priest? Was it because he was engaged before?"

Mark doesn't answer right away.

"It's not really my story to tell, but it might clarify a few things for you. I met Jay when I was twenty-five. We were both on the same international soccer team-"

"What?!" I screech.

Mark smirks.

"Didn't know we were celebrities?" he teases.

"Uh, no. But I wouldn't really call 'professional soccer players' celebrities."

"Tell that to all of David Beckham's fans," Mark rejoins.

"Who?"

Mark looks at me in horror.

"Please tell me that you're joking."

"Um, no. I was pretty much cloistered all my life, remember?"

"But you said that you had internet access!"

"Yeah, where I binge-watched Disney movies."

"Right, well, maybe it's best that you don't know who David Beckham is. Anyway, Jay, Matt, Luke and I were all on the same team because we were drafted from a program for priests in athletics. Because we were playing at a professional level, our vows were put on hold. At the time, Jay was becoming a priest out of spite- not exactly the best reason for joining such a calling," Mark chuckles. "His family really looked down on the profession, considering taking a vow of poverty akin to being tried for a horrible crime. We knew his heart wasn't really in it and when he met a girl at one of the soccer games, we figured 'The Gospel Brothers' was over."

"Did you guys give yourselves that name?" I interrupt.

"No, actually, our fans did. We were a pretty hot commodity since we were becoming priests."

"I can imagine."

And I can. I've seen what's underneath their shirts and I've felt what's in their pants.

"Anyway, Jay met someone. Long story short, they got engaged. All was well until he caught her cheating on him."

"Oh no!" I exclaim. "What a bitch. I hope he sucker punched her right in her cheating twat!"

Mark just shakes his head at me.

"No, and between us, if she hadn't told him that his family was paying her to marry him, I think he might have stuck around."

"I'm sorry, I think I heard you wrong- *his fucking family was paying this skank-hole to marry him?!*"

"Yup, skank-hole was only in it for the money," Mark confirms.

I snort.

"Then her trashy ass didn't see Jay naked, because who the hell would turn their back on his fine-ass dick-"

"Ok! Thank you, Evangeline, I get the picture," Mark coughs. "Although, they did have sex."

"Ugh. Thank God he didn't get whorpes."

"Whorpes?"

"Yeah, herpes from a whore. They're worse than demon herpes."

"Demon herpes?" Mark snorts.

"Yep. But I'd rather take herpes from hell than skank-hole's whorpes."

"Amen to that," Mark jokes and I make the sign of the cross.

Chapter 22

Confessional Sex

"I thought you weren't supposed to leave the convent?" a voice questions behind me.

It's Saturday, and even though twenty-four hours have passed, there's still no word from Jay. I decided that I needed a break and I came over to the chapel to pray. And by pray, I mean smoke. I'm being very diligent because I only have the habit that I'm wearing.

I turn to see Matt making his way towards me.

"I'm praying," I tell him.

He laughs.

"I'm beginning to realize that 'I'm praying' is just your code-word for 'Go away, I'm sinning'."

Now, I laugh.

"You caught me. What are you doing over here?"

He blushes and I feel my eyebrows disappear under my headdress.

"Dude, if your cheeks get any redder, I'm going to be concerned that you might spontaneously combust."

He fidgets at my assessment and my heart goes out to him. I pat the pew that I'm sitting in, beckoning him over. He reluctantly comes to sit by me, but keeps a healthy distance between us.

"Is this because of our kiss or are you mad at me about Jay?" I wonder.

"Definitely that kiss," he says pointedly. "I don't hold you responsible for Jay's decisions."

"So you came over here to pray for the Lord to remove the memory of our kiss from your priestly mind?"

Matt mumbles something unintelligible under his breath and looks away.

Was our kiss that big of a deal-

Then it hits me.

"You came in here to jack off!" I exclaim loudly.

"Evangeline!" Matt hisses, trying to shut me up, but I'm laughing too uproariously.

"Oh my God, you sinner!" I tease. "That's so hot."

More blushing.

I'd be concerned that all the blood in his body is rushing to his head, but I see his dick straining in his black priest pants, so I know a healthy amount is flowing downward, too.

"So, do you always masturbate in the chapel?" I ask conversationally.

He makes a strangled noise in the back of his throat and I smile wickedly at him.

I remember our kiss.

There's so much passion inside of Matt, waiting to burst free.

"I have an idea," I say brightly and Matt regards me suspiciously. "Why don't we do a little chapel bate fest together. Ya know, you show me yours and I'll show me mine."

Matt's face goes carefully blank.

"I. . . don't think that's a good idea, Evangeline."

I scoff at him.

"Of course it's not a good idea! Whoever had any fun with those? This is a baaaaaaaaaaaaad idea. A naughty idea. A *fun* idea," I tease.

I turn sideways in the pew and lift my left leg to rest against the back of it. My right foot is still firmly planted on the floor and I widen my legs and pull my habit over my knee to expose my lace-covered pussy.

Matt is visibly shaking.

"E-E-Evangeline. . ." he tries.

"Yes, Matt?" I ask, stroking a finger up and down my plump outer lips.

I maneuver my panties so that he can get an eyeful as I slowly finger myself.

"Do you like what you see?"

"So pink," he mumbles incoherently, breathing shallowly.

"Now, let me see yours," I instruct, still playing with myself.

Although his eyes look unsure and his hands shake, he unbuckles his pants and pulls out his throbbing erection.

I whimper at the sight of its girthy length, already imagining it filling me up.

Mat strokes himself roughly to the sight of me.

"What are you thinking, Evangeline?"

"That I wish that it was your dick inside of me, instead of my fingers."

He growls savagely and fucking erupts all over his hand, his cum spurting upward.

The sight sends me crashing over the edge and I scream out his name as I come.

When I finally calm down, I look at Matt, who looks like he's in a stupor.

I giggle a little as I crawl over to him and begin licking his hand and dick free of cum.

"Come on," I direct when he still doesn't move.

I grab his hand and walk us over to the confessional booth.

"What are you up to *now*?" Matt wonders.

"If you're going to be a priest, then you need to practice. Go sit down so that you can hear my confession," I order.

I go to the other side and wait.

The confessional has a divider between the priest and the confessor, but the priest can open up the top half for face-to-face confessions. For now, it's shut and I can barely make Matt out through the mesh screen.

"How do I begin?" I ask.

"Forgive me, Father, it's been X amount of time since my last confession," Matt supplies, his breathing still uneven.

Hell, I didn't even tuck back his cock into his pants.

"Forgive me, Father, it's been XXX since my last confession," I purr and Matt half-laughs, half-moans. "I've been a very naughty girl."

I audibly can hear him swallow.

"H-h-how so?' he attempts to speak.

"I've been touching myself. And having impure thoughts. Of a priest. Four, actually," I confess.

Through the shadows, I see Matt reach out to fist himself.

"Go on," he urges.

"I finger-fuck myself every day to the thought of them inside me, filling my pussy, my ass, my mouth, coating me *everywhere* with their cum."

"Oh God, Evangeline, we need to stop," Matt says in panic.

"But Father, I need you to absolve me first," I play-act.

"You filthy little girl, you love this, don't you?"

"Almost as much you love it, *Father*," I murmur seductively.

"And what should we do about this?" Matt asks sternly, finally taking on the role that I know we both crave.

"W-w-whatever you think must be done," I stutter charmingly.

"I'm going to have to assign you a penance," Matt finally rumbles and I have to squeeze my legs together at the sound.

"What should I do, Father? Tell me. I am but yours to direct."

"*Fuck*," he curses and I moan out loud at the sound.

I hear him fumble around until he unlatches the door, then he grasps my hand and drags me over to his side. Without ceremony, he hitches up my habit and pulls me into his lap. I grind my pussy against his dick and he drops his head back.

"Ride me, Evangeline," he orders and I don't even take off my panties.

I push that shit out of the way and slam myself down on his length.

We both groan loudly.

Hopefully, no one comes into the chapel to pray.

They might get an earful of a new kind of prayer.

One that just goes 'Oh God, oh God, oh God'.

I'm so worked up that it takes only a few bounces before I come around his cock, the position pushing and pulling against my clit.

"Shit! Evangeline, get off, I'm going to-"

"I'm protected," I moan, still riding out my orgasm.

That's all it takes for Matt to explode inside of me and I cry out at the feel of his hot cum spurting deep in my pussy.

"Yes, Father. Fucking fill me up," I whimper, and I swear Matt comes some more.

Our harsh breathing is the only sound that fills the confessional as I gently rock in his lap, loving the feel of us combined.

I pull back to give him a kiss.

I pour everything into it: my thanks, my desire, my admiration.

Matt has given me a gift. Not just his virginity, but also his trust.

He didn't second guess me when I told him that I couldn't get pregnant. Hell, even played along with my dirty little fantasy.

And I kind of loved him for it.

"You're going to make a great priest," I whisper against Matt's sweaty, muscled chest and he rumbles out a derisive laugh.

"I just fucked a nun in a chapel, honey, I don't think that is a good indication for my merit as a priest," he says ruefully.

"Uh-huh," I argue. "All the ladies are going to flock to your church to be absolved."

219

Even though I'm joking, he shudders underneath me.

"I don't want to absolve anyone but you then, Evangeline," he whispers and my heart skips a beat at his words.

Chapter 23

Once a Mother, Always a Mother

Sunday is an exhausting day at the convent.

It's our busiest day of the week.

People from the community come in and out all day long.

There are three masses in the morning and one in the afternoon and peppered throughout the day are prayer gatherings and more CCD classes. I do my best to assist my sisters with everything, but I'm a jittery mess.

Matt wasn't at Lauds this morning.

Nor any of the masses.

Just Mark and Luke attended.

A part of me wants to go over and demand where Matt is; but the other part, the cowardly part, stays away from the two remaining Gospel Brothers.

I'm like the Plague.

A total Jezebel.

And I'm going straight to Jeze-Hell.

It's not until the evening, when everyone finally leaves, that Mark is able to corner me.

"Evangeline, we need to talk."

"I didn't mean to fuck him! The temptation was too great! How do you say 'no' to chapel nooky?!"

Wow.

I am the worst.

Mark winces for me.

"This isn't about Matt. What happened between you two is your business. . ."

"But," I urge.

"I failed him," Mark says simply. "He asked me to keep him on the right path and I failed."

I suck in a breath at his words.

"That's ridiculous! You aren't responsible for his actions, or mine!"

"He asked me to be there for him. To guide him back to the path, and I can't."

"Yes, you can," I say firmly. "Remember when you told me people get lost sometimes? They just need a light to show them back to their true path. You are that light, Mark."

"I wish that I was," he murmurs sadly.

"And just why can't you be?" I demand.

"Because Matt doesn't want that light. He said that for the first time, he actually feels alive. That you made him feel this way. He can never go back to living a life without passion and love."

"*Love?*" I say hollowly.

"Love," Mark confirms. "And for that, I can't be angry or upset that Matt has walked away from this life. You didn't take anything from him, just gave him a new direction to go. I just wish it was one with me. I love all my brothers, but Matt. . . Matt's my best friend. I thought we would grow old together and be cantankerous priests."

I see Mark's lips twist at his joke, but it's a sad smile.

"But what will he do now? Did he go to college? How will he get a job?"

I'm rambling again in my worry.

"Evangeline, you don't have to worry about Matt or Jay. Suffice to say they are millionaires. Between what we earned playing professional soccer and with smart investing, they are more than set. And we all have college degrees, too. The church paid for us to go to seminary school, but we also attended business school."

My eyes widen.

Millionaires?

Not that I'm not used to big money.

Walker is a millionaire many times over.

Perks of running drugs, women, and weapons.

I guess that I just didn't expect that kind of money from priests.

"But that's not what I want to talk to you about," Mark continues. "I've, ah, procured an I.D. for you. I've set up a bank account under your new name with enough money for you to start a new life."

I gape at him.

Literally, gape.

With my mouth hanging wide open, I bet I look attractive as fuck.

Not.

"Mark. . ."

I don't know what to say.

No one has ever showed me such kindness, except for Penny, the social worker who really tried to help me.

"It's nothing. Knowing that you're safe is all that matters. Luke is going to take you to a house up north. Rest there for as long as you need and then get out of the state. Maybe head to the east coast. Once there, you should be able to settle down for a bit and get a passport. Then, you can leave the country and start your life anew. Maybe go to Rome and check out if the Vatican has a need for an opinionated tour guide. You can dress up as a nun and tell everyone your heretical ideas," he jokes.

Tears cloud my vision and I leap into his arms, hugging him tightly.

"Thank you, Mark. You'll never know how much this means to me."

He pulls back to look down into my eyes, his whiskey-brown ones full of emotion.

"Go with God, Evangeline."

And then he pushes me away and out of his life.

Luke and Father McMann are waiting for me in the rectory, where Mark directed me to go. When the old priest tries to catch my eye, I look to the ground, biting my lip. Mark told me that he told Father McMann the truth. I'm a little scared of his censure, but I'm terrified of his disappointment. Father and the sisters have really grown on me and I hate that I've lied to them.

"Evangeline?" Father McMann says.

I take a deep breath and finally look into his face.

"Yes, Father?" I ask uncertainly.

He heaves a deep sigh.

"Did you really think you were fooling me or Mother Catherine?" he finally says with a crooked smile.

I gasp and he chuckles in delight.

"H-h-how did you know? Do the sisters know?" I wonder in confusion.

"No, my child, they do not, but both Catherine and I knew Evangeline."

"Then, why didn't you say something?"

I look at Luke in confusion.

Why did Father McMann let me pretend all this time?

He takes my hand and pats it gently.

"Suffice to say that Mother Catherine and I received word from Gabriel."

I see Luke's eyes widen at this announcement.

Who the hell was this woman?

Well, whoever Gabrielle is, I owe her a big thanks.

"I'm sorry about Sister Evangeline. The real one, I mean."

"I am, too. I've been wondering what happened, but Mark filled me in. I'm going to see what is the most tactful way to present this to the police that won't bring anymore hostility and violence to our doorstep. I will be reaching out to the archbishop, but don't worry. It will be addressed. In the meanwhile, we need to get you to safety. Mark said he has a plan. I don't know it. The less this old man knows, the better. You're a sweet child, Evangeline. God has big plans for you, just remember to trust in Him a little."

I smile and hug him.

"Thank you. Oh- who will be the new mother?"

"Do you have any recommendations?" he teases.

"All the sisters are sweet, but I think Mary-Francis or Agnes has the best head on their shoulders for leading the others."

"Very observant. I think you're right. God bless, my child."

"And God bless you, father," I tell him, then I chuckle. "I told a little boy God bless you yesterday after mass when he was leaving with his family. He gave me a funny look and said that he hadn't sneezed."

We all laugh.

"Bye, Father McMann."

"Good-bye, my dear."

I follow Luke out to an unknown car with Wyoming plates.

"Let's get going. We have a six hour drive ahead of us. Oh, your papers are in your seat."

I slip into the passenger side and buckle up.

There's barely any light left in the sky, but I can still make out the name on my new driver's license.

It's says *Evangeline Mater*, and I grin.

Mater is *mother* in Latin.

Chapter 24

Immoral Desires

"Evangeline, wake up; we're here," Luke's voice calls and my eyelids flutter open.

It's night and I have no idea where *here* is.

Luke's tall form is leaning into the car, the passenger door open.

I sleepily reach for my suitcase in the back, but Luke scoops me up, holding me bridal-style.

"I've already taken everything in. Are you hungry?"

"Yes," I murmur, closing my eyes again and resting my head against his firm chest.

"I can order some take-out. What do you like?"

"You."

Luke stumbles and ends up dumping me on the couch.

Thank God that we were in the living room.

"How about some Chinese?"

I yawn.

"Sounds good, but *you* still sounds better."

He gives a strained chuckle and leaves to go order. He comes back a few minutes later.

"I got a sample of a few things."

"Ok. I'm not picky. So, whose house is this?"

"Mark's childhood home."

My eyes widen.

"Are his parents here?" I wonder.

"No, they actually gave Mark this house."

I nod and look around.

Everywhere there are pictures of my favorite guys.

My favorite is the one with the Pope. Matt and Mark are on one side and Luke and Jay are on the other side of the Pope. All five are making some type of silly face. It makes me giggle.

I'm probably going to steal that picture.

"How old are you?" I suddenly ask.

"Thirty-two."

"I'm older," I smirk like this makes a difference.

"I'm taller," is Luke's smug rebuttal and I scowl.

I hate being small.

"I know Mark is thirty-five and if I'm doing my math correctly, Jay is twenty-eight. How old is Matt?"

"Thirty-four."

"And you all came together through soccer?"

"Sort of. Mark and Matt have always been best friends. They entered the seminary together. They're really only nine months apart. It was through soccer that Jay and I ended up meeting Mark and Matt, but I've known Jay for a long time. I was his mentor when he first entered seminary school."

"Oh, cool. And how long have you had a crush on him?" I ask casually.

Luke clasps his hands together and squeezes until his knuckles are white. I reach to gently touch them.

"You don't have to tell me, but I promise there's no judgement."

"I know. And thank you. You'll never know how much that means to me. My family. . ."

He trails off. I scooch closer to him and kiss his hand reassuringly. He takes a deep breath before continuing.

"My parents are very Catholic. I come from a big family with four brothers and three sisters."

I cringe.

"Your mom had eight kids? Her poor vagina," I lament and Luke laughs.

"Well, I'm one of the oldest and my dad caught me looking at some magazines. . . of men," he confesses awkwardly. "I was sent to seminary to purify my soul and consecrate my life to God."

"Um, weren't you over eighteen? Why are you still doing it?"

He shrugs, looking away.

"At the time, I was a people-pleaser and I believed my parents when they said that I was going to burn in Hell. I did it to save my soul. Then I met Jay. . . and I guess I stayed so that I could be with him."

"Oh my God, you love him," I breathe in wonder.

Luke looks me in the face and nods.

"You sweet, generous, kind, gorgeous, giving man," I compliment, then I crawl into his lap before he can protest.

"But you like women?" I query, just to make sure.

Luke grinds his burgeoning length against my ass and I laugh.

"I definitely like women," he reassures.

"Have. . .have you ever done anything with a man?" I ask.

He blushes.

"I wish, but no. You are my first kiss. No one else has ever. . .touched me."

He looks so sad at his confession that I lean in and kiss him.

He shifts me so that I can nestle myself more firmly in his lap and we make out like two teens on their first date. Just as things are getting pretty fast and heavy, there's a knock at the door.

"Fuck, the Chinese," I groan and Luke laughs.

He stands up, but his dick stains against his mesh sport pants.

235

"Do you mind. . . Could you. . ." he attempts and I snicker at his predicament.

He shakes his head at me and hands me some money.

I pay for the food and take it back to the living room, but Luke doesn't make a move for it.

"Are you hungry?"

"Not for food," he finally says and that's all I need to dive right into him, picking up where we left off. I lean into him, tumbling him back until his head rests against the arm of the couch.

I decide to tease him.

"Take off your shirt, I want to see if you're more muscular than Jay. Are you? I assume that you've seen Jay without a shirt. Hell, playing a sport together, I bet you've even seen his cock in the locker room. I wonder if yours will be as thick. I bet it's longer, though."

He moans and whips his shirt off, then kicks his pants off without even having to be asked. His dick strains against his boxers. Without asking permission, I slip them off, taking in the glorious length of his cock.

"Definitely longer. Let me have a taste."

I take him in my mouth and suck, then pulse my tongue on the underside, feeling his dick harden even more.

"Evangeline," he warns.

"Lucas," I growl right back. "Lean back and enjoy. Do you like it when I do this?"

I kiss the tip.

"God, yes. Don't stop!"

I nibble my way up and down his joystick before shifting gears.

"Can I pretty-please ride you?" I faux beg.

"I-I-I don't have any condoms," Luke begins, but I cut him off.

"I can't get pregnant."

Then I whip off my top and unhook my bra. Luke sits up to bury his face in them and I love the feel of his gentle hands and mouth on me. I push him back so that I can take off my pants and underwear. Then, I take his hand and push two fingers inside of me.

He moans so loudly and deeply that you would think it was him getting finger-fucked.

"Oh, Luke, I love the feeling of your fingers inside of me. Does the thought of Jay finger-fucking your ass make you as hard as it makes me wet?"

"Shit. Evangeline," he swears and I giggle.

"Make me come," I beg.

"I don't know how," Luke admits, his face blushing red.

"Keep pumping your fingers into me like you are. I'll play with my clit and you can talk dirty to me. I promise that I'll fucking cum rivets down your arm."

"Dirty talk?"

"Yeah, tell me what you want to do to Jay," I direct.

His dick jerks at my words and his fingers begin a rough and delicious tempo inside of me.

"I want to kiss him while he strokes my dick. I want him to squeeze my balls and let me come in his mouth. I-I-I want to fuck his ass and have him fuck mine."

His words conjure the most erotic imagery and I can't stop the orgasm from crashing over me if I tried. True to my words, I fucking gush all over his hand and I can see the droplets rolling down his arm.

He looks astonished.

"I made you come," he says in surprise and I laugh.

"Yes, you did. Now lick it all up because I'm about to ride you."

He jerks at my words, but licks his fingers, hand, and arm clean of my juices.

"You taste. . . there are no words."

I grin at his honesty and easy manner.

And then I mount him.

His mouth forms a perfect O at my actions. I grab his hands and drag them up to cup my breasts as I gyrate against him. He lasts a hell of a lot longer than I thought that he would, but after a minute or so, he bursts inside of me with a shout.

I get off him to catch some of his cum, licking it daintily off my fingers, before feeding him some.

He blushes.

"Try it. It's delicious. I love licking myself off my fingers after I come," I confess to give him some reassurance.

He leans forward and sucks his come from my hand. I scoop some more for him to try.

"Are you pretending its Jay's?" I whisper naughtily and he grunts.

I kiss him one last time and then we change and eat dinner.

Afterward, we're exhausted and go to bed. Luke surprises me by joining me in my room. There's no hanky-panky, but it's the first time anyone has just *held me*. I feel so safe in his arms. So *loved*. I close my eyes. I don't ever want this feeling to stop.

When I wake up in the morning, he's gone and the hole that's always been in my heart suddenly feels a thousand times bigger.

Chapter 25

A Godsend to the Gut

I'm sure when Mark told me to stay at this house, he only meant for a day or two, but it's now going on four weeks. I can't find it in me to leave. There's pictures of the guys together, on soccer fields, graduating business school, and in the clerical black shirt and pants.

I've decided that I'll take a bus out East in a day or two.

After I get better.

I can't leave because I'm attached to the guys, but I'm also sicker than a dog.

It's the most virulent case of the flu that I've ever gotten.

It's been going on for almost two weeks now.

The body aches and fever are the worst, though.

I know better than to eat anything at this point.

When the weekend passes and I'm still not better, I figure that I need to see a doctor.

I go to the little walk-in clinic some twenty minutes from the house and get myself checked-in. The nurse leads me to a room where I gratefully sit down. After forty minutes, I give up and lay down.

I must have fallen asleep, because when the door opens and the doctor announces himself, I startle so badly, I fall off the side of the damn patient's bed.

"AH! Ouch! Damn you, loud noises!"

"Um, are you alright, Miss Mater?" the doctor asks as he helps me.

"Ugh, I've been better. Sorry, I think I fell asleep and you woke me. I haven't been sleeping very well."

"Well, the flu is not the friendliness of sicknesses. At least you haven't been camping out in the bathroom like most folks that I've been seeing this week."

I shudder.

"I stopped eating days ago," I admit.

The doctor frowns and pinches my arm lightly.

"Ow, hey!" I exclaim, smacking his hand away.

He chuckles at my feistiness.

"I'm just checking to see how dehydrated you."

I grumble.

He could have *asked* first.

"I'd like to run a couple of tests to check your white to red blood cell count and this will tell me if you need an I.V. or not. The nurse will be in to do a quick blood draw and it won't take long to have the results."

"A blood draw? Like with *a needle?* No, thanks, Doc. I'd rather just die."

He laughs at my melodramatics and leaves.

I wasn't joking though. . .

The nurse comes right back in carrying a case and I look at her like she came in with a bloodied chainsaw. This bitch is insane if she thinks that I'm going to let her stick me with anything.

"Has anyone ever told you that you should be a model?"

Her compliment takes me off-guard.

"Ha! I'm on to you! You won't be stabbing me today!" I shout triumphantly, and she looks at me stupidly.

"I'm not going to stab you, ma'am."

"You're not? I thought the doctor said. . ."

"Doctor Patel said that I would be *stabbing* you?"

"Kind of, sort of, not really. . ."

Now I feel foolish.

"Hey, want me to tell you why you shouldn't own and operate a midget brothel?"

She stares at me blankly before erupting with laughter.

It takes her a minute before she regains her composure, but when she's done, she's wiping tears and smeared mascara from her eyes.

"Thank you. I needed that. This job is so joyless. Here, let me see you right arm. You look like you have good veins."

"Um, thanks. That's a weird compliment," I say, but I give her my arm.

She wraps a rubber tourniquet around it tightly.

"Um, wait. What are you doing? I thought that you said you wouldn't be stabbing me?!"

She looks confused again.

244

"I'm just doing a blood draw."

"Yeah, *fucking stabbing me!*"

Realization dawns on her face.

"Oh, you're afraid of needles. Sorry, I didn't have you pegged as trypanophobic. Well, you'll get over that soon. They stick you more than a pincushion when you're pregnant."

Now I stare at her in confusion.

"I'm not pregnant. I just have the flu. Ask the doctor."

"Honey, I have five kids. Trust me, this ain't the flu. That's why we're running these tests."

"No. No! We're running the tests to check my white and red blood cell count. Besides, my tubes are tied!"

She gives me a funny look.

"Of course," she says soothingly. "Now, lie back, relax, and squeeze your hand."

I do as she says.

Sort of.

I think of me being pregnant and I know; I fucking *know* she's right. How in the hell could I have been so obtuse?

All the symptoms are there. . . but my tubes are tied!

There's only, like, a five percent chance that I could get pregnant.

It would be a freaking miracle of God!

Oh shit.

What the fuck was God thinking?

And then I pass out.

I rent a car and drive the six lonely hours back down to San Bernardino.

I'm wearing a baggy hoodie, a ball cap with my hair tucked underneath, and jeans. I know it's foolish to go back, especially *now*, but I need to speak with Mark and the others. When I get into town, I park my rental in a shopping square and get a taxi to take me to The Immaculate Heart of Mary.

It's late, well past nine, when I arrive.

I know all the sisters are in bed, but I ring the buzzer incessantly until a voice inquires who's there.

"It's me. . . ah, Mother Evangeline."

"Mother?" the voice asks and there's such joy in it that my heart aches.

I never got to tell these women good-bye.

The gate buzzes open and I quickly rush inside, checking to make sure no one is watching. Once inside, Sister Mary-Francis is standing there, waiting. She runs over to me and envelopes me into a big hug.

"I told Father McMann that you'd be back. I just knew it. I only took the position as abbess temporarily. I didn't even move into your room. Why are you in street clothes, Mother?"

"It's a long story, Mary-Francis. I need to speak with Father McMann. It's rather urgent, but perhaps you can gather the other sisters and meet me in the basement in a little bit? I need to tell you all something."

She nods and I go through the back of the convent to head outside to the rectory.

Again, I feel terrible knocking on the old priest's door at this hour, but pound until I hear him call that he's on his way.

The look on his face is almost comical when he sees me standing there, antsy to get inside.

"Evange- what? Get inside, child!" he scolds, holding the door open for me and I slip in quickly.

With my usual tact and brilliance, I confess to Father McMann.

"I'm knocked up."

Bless the old guy, he doesn't even blink.

"With Walker's baby?"

Damn, he might be old, but Father McMann has one hell of a memory.

"Um, no," I hedge, not saying more.

"Well, my dear. I know that you were not treated well by the MC, but this child is an innocent. Mark didn't say so explicitly, but I know you were used heinously. His face said it all, so I can only imagine whose child this is, but

Catholics look at pregnancy as a miracle. A blessing. Abortion is frowned upon, except in extreme endangerment of the mother's life-"

"It's one of the Gospel Brothers," I blurt out.

Father McMann stares at me for a long minute.

The longest fucking minute of my life.

"Huh, well, that makes sense," he finally says.

I splutter out a chuckle.

"How the hell does *that* make sense?"

"Language, child. And it makes perfect sense. See, I thought all the others left because John decided not to take his vows. Of the four of them, John had always been the most on the fence about becoming a priest. If his family didn't push him so, I'm not sure he even would have gone to seminary school. Of course, I told the lad that you don't become a priest out of spite, but after his engagement fiasco, I think the priesthood was a balm to his wounded soul. Until you came along, my dear. Now, I see that it wasn't John, but *you* who turned my boys away from this calling."

"At least you still have Mark and Luke," I offer, feeling lower than slug.

"Actually, they left shortly after you; they realized that priesthood wasn't for them either."

"I'm sorry," I mumble, feeling like the priest-stealing Jezebel that I am .

Father McMann flaps a hand at me.

"No need to apologize. If it wasn't God's plan for them to be priests, then he must have something else in mind for them."

I highly doubt God planned for one of the three brothers to knock me up; that seems more like the Devil's work, but I keep my thoughts to myself.

"Now see here, lass. I can see the wheels turning in your head. Don't overthink this. Just get you and that belly blessing to safety."

He turns away and writes something down on a piece of paper.

"I think that you'll find whatever you're looking for here. Now, go tell your sisters good-bye and get back to hiding."

I thank him, hugging him tightly, and then I head back to the convent.

Before going in, I look at the piece of paper.

All that's on it is an address: *Stone's Throw Estate,*
Wilson, Wyoming.

Chapter 26

A Sandy Farewell

Sister Mary-Francis has all the other nuns waiting for me in the basement.

They are snacking on cookies that Sister Rachel made and sipping on hot chocolate. They are so fucking cute it hurts my heart. It hurts my heart even more to have to tell them the truth.

Somehow, I find the gumption.

I don't go into too much detail about the Outcasts of Hell, but I give them the rundown.

"Then, you are in danger and you need to leave," Sister Bernadette announces.

The others nod their heads in agreement.

"Are you guys mad at me for lying?"

Sister Bernadette chuckles.

"I work with teenagers and little kids, trust me, this isn't my first rodeo with liars," she jokes.

"It's not that we condone lying, but we understand why you did it," Sister Mary-Francis tacks on. "I'm truly sorry to see you go, though. You made an excellent abbess."

I laugh outrightly at her absurd compliment.

"I'm not even Catholic. I don't even know the prayers correctly."

"See!" Sister Maria-Concepcion hisses. "I told you that she was saying *'Hail Mary, full of Christ, the Lord is in you'!*"

I look around at them in confusion.

"Isn't that how the *Hail Mary* goes?"

I thought I had that one nailed.

"No," Sister Agnes corrects, "it's *'Hail Mary, full of the Grace, the Lord is with you'.*"

"Well, that doesn't make any sense. Who's this Grace? Since when did Jesus have a sister? And it's 'the Lord is *with* you'? Huh. I figured since Mary was full of him and all pregnant, the line was 'the Lord is *in* you'.

All the sisters laugh at my nonsense.

"We're going to miss you, Evangeline," Sister Agatha says.

"I'm going to miss you all, too. I know I'm not a nun or anything, but. . . I really felt at home here. You made me feel loved and accepted. You still do, even more so now. Thank you for giving me that."

There are a lot of watery eyes when I leave the convent, clicking the gate shut behind me.

I go over to the taxi idling, waiting for me, when a whisper catches my attention.

"Pst! Hey, Rae! Over here!"

I look around in the dark of the night, but I can't see who's calling me. I pinpoint the voice to the bush at the corner of the privacy fence that encircles The Immaculate Heart of Mary.

"Rae!" the voice whisper-yells again. "It's me, Spencer. I need your help! It's my little sister."

Ah, shit.

I wave the taxi off and walk over to the towering shrub.

"Yo, Spencer, I can't see you-"

A powerful hand clamps over my mouth.

"Shut up, cunt."

I freeze, everything inside of me stilling at the sound of Walker's voice.

From the other side of the fence comes Cancer, Reggie, and Aces, Walker's first, second, and third in command.

I look wildly at Spencer.

Of course, he doesn't know about my Belly Blessing, but how could I have been so stupid to endanger it?

Cancer looks over at Spencer and grunts, "Nice work, kid. Now keep real quiet and we won't kill your mom and sister like we did your brother. Now fucking scram."

Before Spencer turns away, I see the hollow look in his eyes and I know.

I know Walker and his crew showed the kid Denny.

Hell, they might have even tortured and killed him in front of the little boy.

The eight weeks that I'd been removed from this world comes crashing back down on me hard.

It's every man for himself out here.

I can't even be mad at Spencer.

He sold me out to save his mom and sister.

And now I'm going to die.

Please, God. Let it be quick.

Walker looks down at me with malice.

"Time for a nap, sweetheart."

Then, he cracks his hand across my face, knocking me out cold.

"Time to wake up, babe," Walker calls, smacking my sore cheek.

I groggily open my eyes, pain exploding in my head and radiating down my body. I'm in bad condition. Walker drags me out of the non-descript van and tosses me onto the sandy ground.

The desert.

This place is like Vegas.

What happens in the desert, stays in the desert.

If I had any doubts as to Walker's intentions, I don't now.

The desert equals death.

"Stealing from me, Raelynn? Of all the people that I thought would betray me, it was never you. But my father warned me. He fucking warned me not to be blinded by a pretty face and a tight cunt, but I was. Your face and pussy haunt my dreams. The fact that I actually have to kill you really pisses me off. Where am I going to find another ass as fine as yours, hmmm?"

I don't bother answering him.

He's just toying with me.

"So, this is what's going to happen. I'm going to fuck you one last time for memory's sake, and then I'm going to let Cancer have a go at you since his piece of ass was a cheating whore and had to be put down. It's really been a depressing couple of months, but we're working through it together. Oh, and then Reggie is going to shoot you in the head. You'll be dead before you even hit the ground."

I shiver at his words, but I know it's the best that I can hope for in this situation, minus the non-consensual sex I'm about to be forced to have with Walker and his dick cousin.

258

Walker strolls around me in a circle, pretending to ponder which hole he wants to fuck on me first. I tune him out. I've had years of practice. I know how to just respond. Physically, I'm doing everything that he demands; mentally, I'm a million miles away.

That is, until Walker pats my ass inquisitively a second time.

There's confusion on his face and I realize it's because he hears something crinkling.

He reaches into my pant's pocket over my right butt cheek and pulls out the piece of paper with the address that Father McMann wrote down.

Panic like I've never known erupts inside of me, spewing forth in a haze of dread.

I've already failed my baby, but I won't fail my boys.

They've done so much for me, and in return, all I did was ruin their lives.

I won't let them die for it now.

Quicker than lightning, I lunge forward and snatch the paper from Walker's hand. Before he or any of the others can react, I eat it.

I fucking swallow that shit whole.

"*What the fuck?!*" Walker roars, and rounds on me in anger.

Cancer follows.

"Now, Reggie!" Aces suddenly screams and then a spray of bullets comes my way.

I slam to the ground in fear.

There's swearing, screaming, and blood.

So much blood.

I shake like a leaf in the wind.

Then the storm calms and there's nothing but silence as the dawn stretches into day across the desert. The hot sun instantly warms the sand and highlights the crimson stains on it. I slowly, and cautiously, roll over. Scanning around me, I see that Cancer and Aces are dead. Both sports bullet holes to the head.

I try not to gag.

I've spent a decade and a half with the Outcasts of Hell, but I genuinely was removed from the brutal violence and murder.

Now, I'm in the center of it.

I look over to Walker, and see him breathing shallowly.

He's been shot in the neck and near his shoulder.

Reggie is in much the same condition.

I doubt either of them make it.

I assess myself and breathe a sigh of relief when I find nothing amiss.

Not saying that I'm going all churchy, but that's a miracle of God.

"Rae," a voice suddenly calls weakly.

Walker.

"Rae, get help."

I stare at the man who took me off the streets. The man who was supposed to care for me. The man who became my biggest nightmare.

"No," I tell him coldly, bending down to collect all the guns.

Like hell am I getting shot because I was stupid and turned my back.

Also, Walker can bleed out in the hellhole.

261

It's kinder than he deserves.

"Rae-Rae," Reggie calls and I look over at him.

I'd always liked Reggie.

"Your attempt to take over the MC failed," I tell him sadly.

He coughs and blood splatters out of his mouth.

"Not trying to do that," he wheezes. "Undercover."

Undercover?

"Don't worry, back up coming," are his final words.

I half-walk, half-crawl over to the van.

Backup is coming.

No sweeter words have ever been spoken.

Chapter 27

The Guardian Cross-Dresser

When backup finally arrives, the sun is at its zenith, and I'm weak and dehydrated.

I'm also afraid for my baby.

A man comes charging out of a black SUV, takes one look at the carnage and starts barking out orders. One of them is to get me inside some air conditioning. I'm set up with some water and the order to rest while an ambulance is sent for.

Another twenty minutes go by before the man comes back to check on me.

"Miss? I'm Detective Marshall. Reggie and Aces were undercover agents in my unit. We've been following Walker and the Outcasts of Hell for some time now, trying to pinpoint their illegal gun-running, among other things. Are you Raelynn Houke, Walker's presumed girlfriend?"

"Yes, I'm Raelynn Houke, but I'm not Walker's girlfriend. I'm not his anything," I spit.

"Of course, my apologies. How long were you with Walker, if I might ask?"

"Nineteen years," I whisper in an aching voice.

"Would you be willing to testify?"

"I'm pregnant," I tell him bluntly. "Can you promise my baby's safety, as well as mine?"

He pauses at this, thinking, before he answers.

"Yes."

"Ok, then I'll testify."

Detective Marshall nods and goes to walk away, but I stop him.

"What took you so long to get here?" I demand.

If they had been tailing us, how the hell did it end in a massacre?

"The tracker lost signal as Walker drove into the desert. If it wasn't for a brilliant tech, we might never have found you."

I shudder.

The enormity of my situation comes crashing down on me.

Alone in the desert with no clue where I was, I'm lucky someone found me.

"I'll have to tell this tech 'thank you'," I joke.

Detective Marshall scoffs.

"I'd like to tell him that myself, but no one seems to know him or be able to find him."

"That's strange," I muse.

"Yeah, well, when we get back to headquarters, if some kid named Gabriel talks to you, send him my way, will ya?"

The detective walks off as the ambulance pulls up.

As they load me into the back of the emergency vehicle, all I can think is that I'm learning loads of new shit lately.

Jesus doesn't have a sister named Grace, and this Gabrielle is apparently a dude.

The hospital room that I'm staying in is at its capacity for visitors, but since they are all nuns and a priest, the staff doesn't say anything. When we got back to San Bernardino and everything checked out for the baby and me, I called the Immaculate Heart of Mary.

Sister Patricia must have broken a record driving everyone to the hospital to see me, but I love having them here. It's nice to have people fawn over me. To care for me.

I grimace when the sisters learn that I'm pregnant and I wait for the lecture, but one never comes.

"Oh, I'm going to start knitting booties," Sister Agatha exclaims excitedly.

"Oh, I just love babies!" Sister Bernadette coos.

I laugh at their obvious joy over the news.

"I need to call Mark," Father McMann announces, but I stop him.

"Wait, Father. I. . . I think that I need to be the one to make that call. They don't know that I was in danger, so it can wait for a moment."

Father agrees, albeit reluctantly.

"Ok, my dear, but don't forget! Now, get some rest. We'll be back tomorrow."

"I'll have those booties! And a blanket, too!" Sister Agatha reassure me and I smile.

I love these nuns.

They leave and my room is blissfully quiet. I start to doze off, when I hear faint knock on the door. I see a young woman in her mid-twenties standing there in a pencil skirt and button-down shirt. Her hair is a gorgeous strawberry blonde and her eyes are bluer than Jay's.

"Raelynn Houke?"

I wince.

I'm not Raelynn anymore.

I'm Evangeline.

"Yes?" I ask tentatively.

"Hi, I'm Nichole Hellman. I'm a social worker. My aunt was Penny Hellman. . ."

The minute she says Penny's name, I recognize her. Even though this is our first meeting, I can see the resemblance between her and her aunt.

"Hi, what can I do for you?"

"Detective Marshall got ahold of me. He mentioned that you wanted to report an incident that happened fifteen years ago. I'm the liaison for the county, working at the court and with the police on these types of cases. When I cross-referenced your name, I realized that my aunt had been the one to place you in that home those many years ago."

"Yes, it was actually your aunt who saved me. The foster family that I had been staying with before were. . . neglectful. Penny took me in and made sure that the family couldn't be foster parents anymore. I stayed with her for a little while. She was so much fun. I didn't realize she had a niece."

"According to your file, you're thirty-three now, so I was only an infant at the time."

"I always wondered what happened with Penny. Why she didn't. . ."

"Why she didn't what?"

"Why she didn't come back to check on me," I say sadly.

"She died shortly after you were put into the Hunts' home."

"Oh, I'm so sorry to hear that!"

"Yeah, my dad was heartbroken. He really looked up to his big sister. That's why I do the work that I do. My Aunt Penny knew the system was broken and she tried to fix it. It got her killed, but damn if she didn't try."

It's on the tip of my tongue to ask how Penny perished, but I swallow my question.

Instead, I ask, "Do you think it's worth it to report the incident since it was so long ago?"

Nichole gives me a hard look.

"Anytime someone touches a child, it should be reported. *Anytime.*"

Her eyes are flinty with determination.

"Mr. Hunt is now in his fifties, but time does not absolve him of his crime," she pauses to give me a look. "Do you know what everyone calls me?"

"Um, Nicki?" I guess.

"Nope. Nickel. See, my Aunt Penny was one tenacious lady, but I'm five times more determined than she was. The system is broken and I'm going to single-handedly fix it."

"Wow, that's. . . a pretty lofty freaking goal."

She chuckles.

"Yeah, my parents always said that I was too strong-willed and stubborn. I prefer indomitable."

"Yeah, I like that one, too. It sounds like abominable, which reminds me of the snowman, and no one fucks with that wintery squatch."

Nichole squints at me before she busts up laughing.

"I like you, Raelynn."

"It's Evangeline, now, actually."

"Oh, cool. Pretty name. It suits you. I'm going to talk with the DA and Detective Marshall and get your case pushed. In the meanwhile, get some rest. The doctors said that you're ok, just a little dehydrated and that you should be out tomorrow evening. Here's my cell number if you need anything at all."

I take the piece of paper from her and it reminds me of the one that I ate.

I need to get out of here and talk to my Gospel Brothers.

They need to know they are going to be fathers after all.

Chapter 28

Doing Jesus a Solid

I'm released from the hospital the next day just as Nichole said, but it takes another five days before I can finally get a rental car and leave. Testifying against the Outcasts of Hell and reporting Mr. Hunt has been an exhausting whirlwind of statement after statement after interview after statement.

But I finally make it.

Thirteen freaking hours and five million pee stops later, I make it.

I have no address, so when I enter Wilson, I go to a gas station for directions.

And another pee break.

This freaking baby inside of me must be using my bladder as a body pillow or something.

First thing that I'm going to do after I give birth is hold it. I'm not going to pee for hours on end.

I walk into the gas station and up to the clerk who's fiddling on his phone.

"Hi, excuse me. Do you know where Stone's Throw Estate is?"

"Yeah, it's a few miles outside of town," he responds, not even looking up from his phone.

I wait, but he doesn't say anything more.

"Which direction?"

No answer.

"Hello? HELLO!"

He finally looks up with bloodshot eyes.

"Ugh, are you fucking high?"

"As a kite," he parries. "It's the only way I can keep myself going."

"Wow, well that's depressing as fuck."

"All I've got is this dead end job."

I put on my Mother cap.

"Well, be thankful that you have one. And if you hate it so much, fucking get a new one, dude."

"What would I do?"

I feel like 'try to own and operate a midget brothel' is *not* the correct answer right now.

Suddenly, an idea comes to me.

"You can be a priest!" I tell him excitedly.

I took four good men from the church, the least I can do is give one shitty dirtball back in return.

The clerk crinkles his nose at me.

"Don't you have to be Christian or some shit to be a priest?"

"Catholic, which is a part of Christianity. Wow, look at you knowing this stuff already. I bet you make a way better priest than I did a nun," I praise.

"You were a nun?" he squints.

"Yeah, until I got knocked up by some brothers, who I'm trying to find to tell them that they're going to be fathers. So, if you could clarify your directions, I would appreciate it."

The poor kid just blinks at me, but manages to send me off the way that I need to go.

I leave the gas station feeling refreshed.

I might not be a Mother anymore, but I'm still spreading peace, love, and all that other hippy shit around.

Just as the kid said, about five miles outside of town, two cobblestone pillars on the left come into view. One of the pillars has a plaque with the name 'Stone's Throw Estate' on it. I turn down the drive, thinking of what to say when one of the guys opens the door. Luckily, it's a long-ass driveway because everything that I'm coming up with is bad.

When the house finally comes into view, I almost veer off the road.

Which is a damn good thing that I didn't, because I would have gone right into the stream that runs in front of the massive home.

It's a legit mansion.

And these four were going to take vows of *poverty?*

The house seems to go one forever and it's a gorgeous blend of cobblestone, wood, and floor-to-ceiling windows. I drive past the carriage house, the pool house, and up to the front doors. I get out and nervously ring the doorbell.

Would a butler or housekeeper answer the door?

What should I say to them?

I'm so busy pondering this new conundrum that when the door does open, I'm not expecting Mark to be on the other side.

"Evangeline?" he asks in surprise.

"I think that we should have sex," I blurt out and then cringe. "I didn't mean to say that."

Mark laughs.

"I think my favorite thing about you is that you say *exactly* what you mean."

I stick my tongue out at him.

"I do not. If I really spoke my mind, I would have said that I want you to put back on your clerical clothes, bind my hands with a rosary, and fuck the sin right out of me."

Mark's eyes widen only slightly.

"Excuse me, for a moment, please," he says politely, before shutting the door in my face.

"Hey!" I yell through the glass panes as I watch him walk away.

He isn't gone for long.

He comes striding back with three other men in tow.

My other three Gospel boys.

Mark reopens the door, but no one says anything and I huff angrily.

"Well, isn't someone going to inv-"

My words are cut off by Jay, who continues walking right past Mark, up to me and physically scoops me into his arms. Before I can even process what's happening, his mouth is over mine and I'm on fire. I wrap my legs around his torso and throw myself into the kiss.

It's a bittersweet moment.

The kiss is full of regret, happiness, apology, desire, and most importantly, *love*.

Jay finally breaks the kiss and his ragged breathing matches mine.

"Later. I promise that we'll continue *later*, but go say hi to the others," he directs and my toes curl at his promise.

I launch myself into Luke next, kissing him with a little more reserve.

Then Matt.

Finally, I turn back to Mark, feeling awkward.

He doesn't reach for me, but beckons me inside.

"Come on in," he finally invites and I step into the impressive home.

Holy shit, I can't even with this place.

Without waiting for a tour, I simply make myself at home and meander around. From the foyer, I follow a hall into a large library with giant bay windows. It's like reading heaven. Next, I follow my nose to the large kitchen. There's a walk-in pantry and a freaking wine cellar. It's fully stocked, and all I can think is that I can play a lot of naughty games with my Gospel boys and that much wine.

There's a formal dining room, an informal one, a sitting room, and a living room.

Apparently, there's a difference between the last two.

Matt and Jay make comments here and there; Luke is silent, as usual, and Mark. . .

I don't know what Mark is, but it's unsettling how he follows without a word.

He remains a few paces behind us, detaching himself from our group and I can't help but wonder if it's his way of saying that he doesn't want to be a part of whatever we have going on.

Chapter 29

Father Cock Block

Jay leads me into the living room for us to sit and talk.

"Ok, now, why are you here?" he asks gently.

"Don't you want to know how I even found you?"

Mark laughs mirthlessly from across the room where he's propped against a wall. His muscles strain in the simple white t-shirt he's wearing and my mouth waters.

Down, girl.

"We know how you found us. Father McMann gave you the address. So, that leaves *why* are you here? You are supposed to be in hiding," Mark says.

The censure in his voice is obvious and I don't know if it's because I'm not in hiding or because I potentially brought my troubles to their fancy-ass doorstep.

I hesitantly tell them everything that's happened, minus my belly blessing.

The happy countenances of Jay and Matt evaporate and all the guys wear angry frowns by the time that I'm done.

"Walker is dead?" Mark asks softly.

"Yeah, he passed before the ambulance could get there."

"Good," he says with conviction and my eyes widen in shock. "One less asshole this world has to deal with."

"Hear, hear," Jay agrees.

"What the fuck is wrong with you two? That's not something priestly to say!"

"We're not priests," Mark points out dryly.

"You know what I meant," I scowl.

I turn around in exasperation and gasp.

Over the fireplace is a large painting of a beautiful man. He is tall and broad like Luke, but has Jay's golden hair with Mark's soft curl. His eyes are a vibrant green, but have Matt's flecks of gold and brown, too. He's like all four of my Gospel boys made into one hot-ass man.

"Who's *he*?" I ask to no one in particular.

"That's Gabriel," Matt says and I swivel around so fast that I fall over onto a sofa.

"WHO?!"

All the guys are looking at me like I've lost it.

"Gabriel, the archangel of the Word of God? Spreader of the Good News? Patron to the Gospel writers and all evangelists?" Luke answers questioningly.

"Why is she a he?!" I screech.

"He's always been a. . . *he*," Mark says slowly, but Jay begins to chuckle.

"The name is *Gabriel*. Not *Gabrielle*," he corrects and I feel myself blush.

I've only ever heard Gabrielle.

Now everything is clicking. Sister Evangeline's words, Detective Marshall's mystery tech who saved my life. . .

They were *him*.

"Why do you have a picture of him?" I ask, feeling overwhelmed.

"Because he's *our* patron, our guardian. We're the Gospel Brothers, this generation's evangelists."

"And I'm Evangeline," I breathe, realizing the connection.

"And you're Evangeline," Jay repeats, his voice a deep timbre of emotion.

We stare at one another, a confession trembling on both our lips.

"Evangeline, I love you-"

"I'm pregnant."

Mark slips from the wall and stumbles into the piano in the corner. Matt spits out the water that he had just taken a drink of. Luke's mouth forms a perfect O of surprise, and Jay. . .

Jay looks confused.

"How. . . how did this happen?"

"How the hell do you think it happened?" Mark snaps, straightening himself once more. "This is what happens when you fuck."

His crude words and harsh tone make me shrink back into the couch.

"Enough!" Matt orders fiercely. "You're upsetting Evangeline."

Jay isn't put off by Mark's words, though.

"I know how babies are made, you dick," comes his rebuttal and I almost choke.

I've never heard him speak like this.

"But Evangeline had her tubes tied when she turned eighteen."

Luke, Matt, and Mark look at me in shock.

"Why would you do that?" Luke wonders and I give him a look.

"Do you really think that I had a say in that? And besides, I wasn't in any position to bring a kid into the world. Hell, I'm still not. I don't even know which of you is the father!"

"Well, we know it's not me," Mark bites out bitterly.

"Thank the Baby Jesus, this might mean the kid doesn't have your piss-poor attitude," I snarl right back.

Luke coughs.

"Are you two done?"

"NO!" we both childishly yell at the same time.

Luke laughs.

"Listen, Evangeline, why don't you bring your bags in and we can get you settled in a guest room? Maybe you can shower and rest and we can all go out to eat tonight. Something to soothe our frazzled nerves."

"A bar sounds great," I agree wholeheartedly.

Matt frowns, but I see the smile lurking within it.

"He said 'out to eat', not 'out to drink'. Besides, you can't drink, remember?" he reminds pointedly looking at my flat stomach.

Ugh.

That's right.

No booze until after I give birth.

This is going to be a miserable nine months.

Luke, Jay, and Matt lead me out of the room. I chance one last look behind me and catch Mark staring holes into the back of my head. I glare right back and leave. The other three show me to a beautiful room in soft gray tones. They bring in my bag and treat me like a fucking princess.

I love it and adore them for it, but I kind of want them to treat me like a whore instead.

Maybe if I wear something naughty for dinner. . .

I'd gone shopping weeks before and bought basic clothing necessities, but there was one little number that I couldn't resist. A white, one-shoulder mini dress. The color looked so innocent against the tight silhouette of the body-hugging fabric that I couldn't resist.

I also bought teal pumps, some turquoise and gold jewelry, and a flimsy lacy bra and pantie combo.

I take a nice long shower and then do my makeup, really playing up my light green eyes and keeping my lips neutral and glossy. I let my hair dry on its own and it tumbles in curly waves all around my shoulders and down my back.

Then, I slip on the dress over my perfumed body and lacy undergarments, followed by the pumps and the jewelry.

When I look in the mirror, a total knockout looks back.

Those good boys aren't going to know what's hit them when they see me.

I saunter down the halls to the living room, where everyone is waiting for me. The sun has set and the room is aglow with soft lamp-light. Matt and Jay are standing by the coffee table, looking at something on someone's phone and Luke is over by the piano, swirling a drink in a tumbler glass.

Mark is noticeably missing.

The other three are all dressed in nice slacks and button-down shirts.

It makes me want to rip their shirts open and lick them all over.

If I lick them, that makes them mine, right?

I step into the room and the click of my high heel gets everyone's attention.

And when I say *everyone's attention*, I mean their dicks.

These pants hide *nothing*.

I need to find out where they bought them and buy them six more pairs each for Christmas.

I walk over to Jay and Matt, rubbing my hands over both their cocks.

They're so hard and I'm so fucking wet.

I have the perfect solution for all our problems, too.

I turn so that my back is to them, still continuing to stroke their dicks, but *now* I can watch Luke. I smile hungrily at my tall loner and he groans.

Oh man, I'm going to ride them so-

"Evangeline?" Mark's voice calls and I swear I jump a foot in the air.

Guilty, I yank my hand away from Matt's and Jay's glorious erections.

"I wasn't doing anything! I was just checking them for ticks-"

I pause in the middle of my lame-ass excuse.

Mark is standing there, fully dressed in the black pants and shirt of a priest, minus the clerical collar.

That's in his hand.

"Evangeline, we need to talk."

I grimace and balk.

"Ah. . . can it wait until after dinner?"

And sex, I add mentally.

"No," he says sternly, causing butterflies to erupt in my stomach at the sound.

Dammit, now's not the time, hormones. It's a shit-show out here! Get it together!

"We'll wait outside for you two," Matt says lightly and he and the other two leave me alone with Mark.

"I've made a very important decision, Evangeline, and I think that you should know," Mark announces, slipping the white clerical collar in place.

Oh.

Fuck.

Chapter 30

Father Knows Best

MARK

I try to keep my countenance stern as I look at Evangeline, but it's a struggle.

She's wearing an itty-bitty white dress that only covers one arm and leaves little to the imagination. Her olive-complected skin practically glows in the soft lamp-light and her legs look miles long in the teal heels.

Her hair is a mess of curls that has me wanting to grab them and drag her to do my bidding.

I take a deep breath to get control over myself.

"Y-y-you became a priest?" Evangeline whispers in shock.

"I prayed for a long time on this and asked God to give me guidance as to what I should do. Thankfully, the

Lord directed me down the right path. Now, it's time to talk about *you*."

"*Me?*" she sputters. "What about me?"

"Oh, please, Evangeline. Don't play coy with me. You've been a very sinful woman. Do you not think my brothers told me what you did with them?"

She blushes becomingly and my cock twitches at the sight.

"Do you not think Matt told me about your playacting? In a chapel, no less?"

"I-I-I can explain," she attempts and I snort.

"I would like to see you try."

Now, she glares at me.

"It doesn't matter now. They're not becoming priests," she pouts and I step to walk around her.

She clutches her necklace nervously as I circle her.

"And that upsets you, doesn't it? You liked it when they were becoming priests. You *got off to it*, didn't you?" I accuse and she takes a ragged breath.

"I didn't-"

"What did I say about lying?!" I thunder and she jumps at my words. "Go kneel on the prayer bench."

I point to it in the corner of the living room and she walks unsteadily over. She gracefully gets to her knees.

"Lean forward and fold your hands together so that we may pray," I command.

Another glare starts to form and I growl at her. A whimper escapes her sealed lips, but I know it's not from fear. I walk over and pull a scarf from my pocket.

"What are you doing?" she asks in surprise when I tie it over her eyes, blindfolding her.

"You are too inattentive. Without your vision, you can now focus on my words. You don't need to worry about what's going on around, but rather, what's going on inside of you. Praying is much like meditation. You need the correct mindset to do it effectively."

I stare at her for a moment, drinking in the sight of her blindfolded and on her knees. This time, I don't try to corral my thoughts or my dick. I run a hand roughly over the length of it through my pants.

"M-M-Mark?" she stammers uncertainly.

"Yes, Evangeline?" I whisper hotly in her ear, as I come to kneel down behind her, my legs bracketing her body between them.

"What are you doing?!" she asks in shock, rearing against me.

"I am helping you pray. Now, hold still," I command harshly.

I sound like a dick, but I know she loves it.

"Now, begin saying the 'Our Father'."

Her words come out stilted and uneven.

I run a finger down her spine and her hands fly apart to grip the wood.

"Keep your hands folded," I snarl, but she makes no move to obey me.

"I see that we have a listening problem, but I can take care of that."

I reach behind me and pull out a sturdy wooden rosary; then, I clasp her hands together while I wind it around them. Her breathing is coming in soft, shallow puffs and I know she's finally realized my game.

"M-M-Mark?" she asks once more.

"It's *Father* to you," I hiss and she moans sexily.

"Yes, Father," she obeys and my cock can't get any harder.

"Now, why are you praying?"

"Because I've been a bad girl."

"Very good," I praise. "Tell me, what has my naughty little girl done?"

She sucks in a breath at my words and then tells me *every* dirty thing that she did with my best friends.

I lied.

My dick can get harder.

Painfully so, in fact.

I push her dress up over her perfect ass before bending down to run my tongue over it and her pussy. I see it quiver and I tear the lace underwear clean off her body.

"So, you want us to fuck you in all your holes?" I inquire when she finishes.

"P-p-please, Father. Yes."

The sound of her begging makes my head swim.

"I'm going to fuck you and I want you to pray like you've never prayed before. Do. You. Understand?" I ask savagely, pulling my aching cock from the confines of my black pants.

"Yes, Father!" she shouts and I slam into her tight pussy from behind.

Instantly, her heat floods me enveloping me whole, and I pause so that I don't fucking unleash my load deep inside of her.

"I don't hear any praying!" I bark, stalling.

She opens her mouth as I start jackhammering into her perfect warmth, and I almost laugh at the rambling words she's trying to string together into a prayer. I fuck her fast and hard, her pussy not even coming close to what I imagined.

It's so much more.

This is my Heaven.

"Oh God, Father! I'm going to come!" she announces.

"Don't even fucking think about it," I snarl, yanking her head back with a fistful of her hair. "I. Will. Tell. You. When. You. Can. Come."

Her whimpers are the only sound that fill the room as she struggles to contain her orgasm.

I know that she can only hold on so much longer, and I'm on the edge, too.

"I don't hear any praying," I reprimand and it takes everything for her to start again.

I feel her pussy clamp down on me just as my orgasm comes barreling down and out through my balls.

"COME FOR ME, EVANGELINE!" I roar.

"AMEN!" she screams as her pussy milks my cock dry.

Afterward, we just kneel there, trying to catch our breaths. Eventually, I unbind her and take off the blindfold. When she looks at me, her eyes are large and full of emotion.

"I love you, Mark. I love you all so much it fucking hurts."

"I know, baby. I love you, too."

"Thank you. . . for this. It was. . .wow."

I laugh at her wording.

"So, you're not really a priest?" she asks for clarification.

"No," I promise. "This is just for when you've been bad and need to be put back in line."

She bites her lip at my words and my cock stirs again.

"I think that I might have forgotten some things," she admits coyly.

I shake my head in mock resignation.

"Whatever shall we do with you, Evangeline?"

"Well. . . you didn't spank me. . ."

Sweet Lord, I'll never be able to get enough of this woman.

Chapter 31

Virtuous Blackmail

We settle into a routine and before I know it, I've been living with the guys for three weeks. I still check in daily with Detective Marshall on an encrypted email server, but he reassures me that these things take time and I won't be called to testify until long after the baby is due.

I'm now padding into the kitchen for a late afternoon snack, when I hear a knock at the door.

I walk to it and see Father McMann through the window panes.

With a big smile, I open the door to welcome him.

"Father! Wel-"

"Are the boys here, lass?"

His abrupt tone takes me off guard.

"Yes, they're in the living room bickering about God knows what."

"Good," the old priest grunts and marches into the house like he owns it.

He makes his way to the living room, where all four guys are arguing about some theological dogma. I don't even know what the topic is, but I already have a headache.

You can take the men from the priesthood, but you can't take the priest out of the men, apparently.

At least they leave that shit outside of the bedroom.

Usually.

Unless "Father Mark" is visiting.

I giggle at my naughty thoughts and Father McMann looks at me sharply.

"This is no laughing matter, my child. You are living in sin, with not one, but four men! What do you plan to do to rectify this?"

"Um, keep it a shameful secret until everyone finds out and then tell them to fuck off?" I offer.

My Gospel boys groan at my crass answer, but I mean it.

My life, my choices.

I've spent too much time letting other people dictate to me how to live it.

"I believe that I have the answer you're looking for," Mark says, and I glare at Father McMann in annoyance.

"If there was a correct answer, why did you even bother asking me?" I say in a huff.

Of course, he doesn't say anything.

Mark walks over to the piano and lifts the back.

"What. . .why the hell is this full of shit?!" he roars.

"Language, son!" Father McMann reprimands and I smile evilly.

I'm the best worst influence *ever.*

I realize that Mark is glaring at me, waiting for an answer.

"What?! I thought it was a place to store stuff," I defend.

"It's not a drawer, Evangeline," Mark snarks.

"Then why did I see *you* put something in there?"

"That was different. . . I was hiding something important."

"I was, too," I announce loftily, crossing my arms over my chest.

"What?" Mark demands right back.

"Luke's healthy shitty recipes," I confess.

"Hey!" Luke cries.

He's our resident chef, but has taken it upon himself to make sure that I eat the cleanest, purest food.

I told him that was bordering on religious fanaticism and to knock it the fuck off.

No one needed to be *that* pure.

"No wonder all I can find are dessert recipes," Luke grumbles.

"Yeah, well, I literally have an asshole growing inside of me. Forgive the fuck out of me if I think that I deserve some cookies for it."

"Did she just call our kid an asshole?" Matt asks in disbelief.

"No," Mark clarifies, "she's saying that their rectum is growing inside of her."

Jay shoulders shake.

"Rectum," he bursts out, busting up at the word like a ten-year-old.

And fuck if I don't giggle right alongside him.

"Sphincter," I wheeze.

"Prostate," he parries.

"Taint."

"Anus."

"Hershey highw-"

"Are you two done?" Father McMann queries dryly.

"Yes, sorry, Father. Mark, you were going to reveal something from the not-drawer piano?"

He sighs heavily, but pulls out a piece of paper and hands it to me.

It's a legal document, notarized by the state of Wyoming.

Upon closer inspection, it's a name change.

"You changed your name?" I ask Mark quizzically.

"Yes."

"*Marcus Matthew Lucas John Brothers?* You don't think that's-"

My question fizzles out when I notice him bending down on one knee.

Luke, Matt, and Jay all follow suit.

"Evangeline," Luke begins, "You are our heart."

He hands me a gorgeous gold heart pendant studded with diamonds.

"You are our sun," Jay continues and hands me an earring.

"And our moon," Matt adds, handing me the other earring.

It's a sun and moon entwined and the eyes are twinkling sapphires.

"You are our life," Mark says before I can study the jewelry more. "Will you marry us?"

And from his back he pulls out a black ring box. Nestled inside is a gorgeous princess-cut diamond surrounded by one ruby, one sapphire, one emerald, and one topaz.

Mark, Luke, Matt, and Jay.

And I'm their diamond in the rough in the middle.

"OH MY GOD!" I suddenly squeal. "You're all marrying me?"

"Why do you think Mark changed his name, lass? Has pregnancy addled her brain?" he asks the guys and I mock glare at him.

"But. . . doesn't the Church, you know. . . frowny face that?"

"Disapprove, you mean? Yes, but it's more of a legality issue. You can only legally have one husband. Mark changed his name so you could marry them all."

"AWWWW! I'm going to become Mrs. Brothers!"

I laugh at the last name that Mark chose.

"But Father, do you. . . approve?"

"Dear, I wouldn't have given you their address if I didn't approve. Now let's get you dressed. This old man isn't as young as I was last week. I need a nap from all that driving."

Father McMann comes with me and helps me pick out something to wear.

Of course, my new jewelry adorns my ears and neck.

And soon the ring will follow.

After I get dressed and sweep my hair into an updo, I stop my favorite priest in the world.

"I have a favor to ask, please."

Ten minutes and a pee break later, Father begins the ceremony.

It takes place against the backdrop of the setting sun and the wilderness to the West. I couldn't have asked for a more gorgeous moment to get married, and my heart swells as I walk toward my men.

I'm wearing the black leggings and white tank top with the words 'Team Spirit' that they gave me many moons ago.

It's the first gift anyone has ever given me without strings attached.

I take my place to Father McMann's right and he begins.

It's short and sweet, exactly how I would have planned my wedding if I had known that I was getting married.

"And do you, Evangeline Mater, take Marcus Matthew Lucas John Brothers to be your lawfully wedded husband; to cherish, love, and honor; in sickness or health, until death do you part?"

"I d-"

"That's not right, Father," Mark interrupts my vow and I glower at him for cutting me off. "It's love, honor, and obey."

Father McMann lets out a cough.

"Evangeline asked that I take that part out."

"Oh," Mark says. "Who would have thought she would have a problem with the word 'obey'? I know the other night she didn-"

"Marcus Matthew Lucas John Brothers! That's enough!" I howl and everyone laughs.

"Alright, don't interrupt her this time. Lass, your answer?"

"I do," I say with unwavering conviction, looking each of my men in the eyes.

"And do you, Marcus Matthew Lucas John Brothers, take Evangeline Mater to be your lawfully wedded wife; to love, honor, and obey; in sickness or health, until death do you part?"

"Hold on! How come we have 'obey' in our vows?" Mark demands to know.

"She told me that I couldn't be the godfather *or* perform the baptism if I didn't say the vows just so," Father McMann confesses.

"You let a fake nun blackmail you?" Matt asks incredulously.

"She's a wily one. And tenacious. I'd watch out for her," the old priest warns, and I snicker. "Now, your answer, son."

Mark glares at me as he says, "I do."

I laugh in delight.

This marriage is already off to a perfect start.

"Excellent, I now pronounce you men and wife. You may kiss the bride."

Jay swoops in before anyone else and claims my mouth. Matt yanks me from him to give me a kiss with a little too much tongue. Luke's kiss is sweet and chaste and

Mark's reminds me of how he devoutly defiled me the other night.

"Now to consummate the marriage!" I joke.

Father McMann groans.

"Wait until I've gone back to the carriage house first, please."

"You mean you don't want to see a fake nun have a gangbang with four ex-priests?"

"MAY GOD BLESS YOU!" Father McMann yells, leaving us to our newly married devices.

Chapter 32

Fucked Seven Ways To Sunday

"Meet us in the master bedroom," Mark directs and I sprint off to my room to change.

Holy shit.

Holy shit.

I'm going to have my first five-way.

I change into something super classy: heels, thigh highs with a garter belt, and bra.

Fuck underwear.

I don't need that crap for this five-way.

I make sure my hair is down.

I know how much my guys love having something to pull.

I take one last look in the mirror, placing a gentle hand on my softly rounded stomach. It's still barely even noticeable, but I swear that I can feel something fluttering inside of me from time to time.

"Let's go love on your daddies," I giggle to my tummy as I head back to the master bedroom.

When I go back inside, I almost stumble to my knees. Of course, I shouldn't be surprised because my guys love role-play almost more than I do, but Matt and Mark are dressed in their clerical black, and Jay and Luke are wearing their old soccer uniform.

I lick my lips.

Fuck, they look delicious.

"She's not wearing underwear," Luke remarks. "How does she expect us to last when she's not even covered?"

I grin.

Good.

They were just as rattled as me.

"Come here, Mrs. Brothers. We need help stretching," Jay directs.

I walk over to stand between the two men and sink to my knees, my ass resting on my heels.

"How can I help you stretch?" I ask coyly, running my hand up and down both their dicks.

"That's a good start," Jay rasps.

I yank their silky mesh shorts down and praise Jesus and all the saints, they aren't wearing anything underneath.

I take turns between stroking them with my hand and fucking them with my mouth. Every so often, I tug one forward a smidge; eventually, their dicks are only centimeters apart.

I look back up to them as my tongue teases both the tips of their dicks at the same time- that's how close together they are. Suddenly, an idea takes root, and before I can fully analyze my intentions, I lean back to rub Jay's and Luke's dicks together.

Both are slippery with pre-cum, and I love watching the shiny smoothness stroke over one another.

Jay's eyes are still closed in ecstasy, but Luke opens his and sees what I'm doing. His eyes widen in shock and he garbles something in panic. This causes Jay to open his. Like Luke, Jay is surprised and he reaches out an arm to brace it on Luke's shoulder, groaning.

This is Luke's undoing.

With a shout, he comes all over Jay's dick and my hand.

I moan so loudly; everyone stops to look at me.

"Fuck, that was so hot," is all I can manage as I lean in to lick Luke off of Jay.

"Yeah, it kinda was," Jay rasps in pleasure.

Luke gasps.

"You. . . you aren't upset?" he asks hesitantly.

"About what? Clearly, our girl loves it," Jay smirks.

Luke stares at him before asking, "How long have you known?"

Jay chuckles.

"I know you think that you were being discreet, but I've *always* known. It didn't matter then, and it doesn't matter now," Jay vows.

Luke looks like he wants to cry.

Instead, he pulls Jay forward and kisses him deeply.

At the same time, I reach under Jay's dick and squeeze his balls hard while pushing gently against his taint.

This time, Jay is the one to give a surprised yelp as he comes all over Luke's dick. When I look up, poor Jay appears dazed and I giggle. I swipe a finger through his cum, tasting it.

"Mm-mm, try some, Luke, " I direct, as I get up and walk over to my naughty priest husbands.

Both look a little stunned at the turn of events, but their cocks strain in their black pants.

They enjoyed the show, but I know both don't swing like Jay does.

"You two enjoy each other and the show," I wink at Jay and Luke when I'm positioned between Matt and Mark.

Matt is at my back and Mark is in front.

"How do you want this, babydoll?" Matt inquires.

"Hard, fast, and rough as fuck," I say huskily.

"Then climb up and do as you're told," Mark commands.

"Yes, Father," I answer.

I hook my legs around his waist and he effortlessly picks me up.

We kiss for a long minute, until I feel Matt at my back, pressing into me. I love being sandwiched between these two strong men.

"Do you have the lube?" Mark asks Matt and I feel my ass clench in anticipation.

"Right here, brother," comes his reply. "But first. . ."

I strain my neck to see what he's doing.

Matt unzips his pants and frees his cock.

My mouth goes dry at the sight.

"Fuck, I forgot how big you are, Father."

His dick pulses at my words.

I scramble off of Mark so that he can undo himself, too.

In the meanwhile, Matt has taken a generous amount of lube and he's gently working his fingers into my asshole.

"Jesus, she's tight," he moans.

"Imagine how tight she's going to feel with both of us in her."

The whole room erupts in a chorus of groans at his words.

Once Mark is free, I waste no time climbing back up and seating myself over his dick.

"Fuck, I forgot how good you feel," Mark whispers into my ear.

"Not nearly as good as you feel, Father," I manage to whimper.

Mark jogs me up and down his thick erection before pulling me into his chest and spreading my ass cheeks. Matt positions himself there and I feel his dick rub against me.

"We'll go slowly" he promises, feeding the tip of his dick into my ass.

I breathe through the sensations bombarding my body and I've never felt so full. After a minute or so, he's fully seated inside of me. Neither mock priest moves and I nearly burst into tears.

"Please. *Please, Fathers!*"

This stirs them into motion and in perfect timing, they fuck me just like I asked. Rough, hard, fast, and it's so fucking hot. I don't last long.

I convulse around them in an orgasm that crosses my eyes, but they aren't finished.

Over and over and over they slam into my receptive body; I come three times before both unleash inside of me.

A shout draws my attention and I see Luke on his knees in front of Jay, swallowing him whole. Luke's dick is twitching as he comes all over the wood floor.

The sight sends me over the edge again, and Mark groans against the tightening of my pussy around his cock.

"That. . . was. . . fucking. . . amazing," Matt manages to say.

"Yes, it was," Mark agrees. "Let's set her down. We don't want to squish the baby."

I crinkle my nose at his words, then laugh when something occurs to me.

"What's so funny?" Mark demands.

"Well, since I'm pregnant and we all just had sex, I guess that makes you all a bunch of motherfuckers!"

Epilogue

Angelic Fate

I give birth on a blustery Spring day in late March. The wind howls, but not as loudly as I do. The whole wing is full of nuns, a priest, and four anxious men. This is the most blessed place in all of the hospital, I swear.

It takes six long hours, but I finally pop out a baby boy.

The nurses assess him, weigh him, takes his prints, and then bring him back to me. They haven't added the ointment to his eyes and he stares at me with wonder on his little face. I stare back in the same awe. He has a headful of jet-black hair, just like Luke.

But it's curly.

Just like Mark's.

His face is serious as he considers me and I quirk a smile at his eyes.

319

One is bright blue, like Jay's, and the other is a hazel green, like Matt's.

He reminds me of the portrait of the guardian angel in the den.

"I'm going to name you Gabriel," I whisper to my newest little man.

"That's perfect," Jay agrees as my other favorite men come striding into the room.

We decided four men in the delivery room would have been chaotic, so I birthed this babe solo, but I'm so relieved to have them by my side again.

"You think so, too?" I ask.

"I do," Matt concurs. "It's more than perfect, actually."

"It's fate," Luke interjects.

I chuckle at their superstition.

"And why is it 'fate'?" I tease.

"Because today is the feast day of St. Gabriel the Archangel," Mark replies and I feel my face blank.

Well, fuck me.

I guess it is fate.

Four months later, I was called to testify against the Outcasts of Hell.

Two months after that, I went to court against Mr. Hunt *and* Mrs. Hunt.

And won.

The most satisfying thing: the Hunts were stripped of their privileges as foster parents and the children living with them at the time were immediately removed. A full scale investigation was conducted to see if further abuse and sexual assault was committed.

After that, Raelynn Houke and my past were officially laid to rest.

Before I left to go back home with Gospel hubbies, Nichole got ahold of me.

She had found Spencer for me.

She promised to get his mom, sister, and him out of Del Rosa and to a safer neighborhood.

321

Spencer is now attending school on the other side of town and has a weekly therapist to help him over his trauma.

Mark is teaching at a seminary school nearby our home in Wyoming.

Jay is going to law school.

And Matt and Luke stay home and help me with the baby for the time being.

As for me, well. . .

I'm living the motherfucking dream.

The End

Father Hotness Has a Message

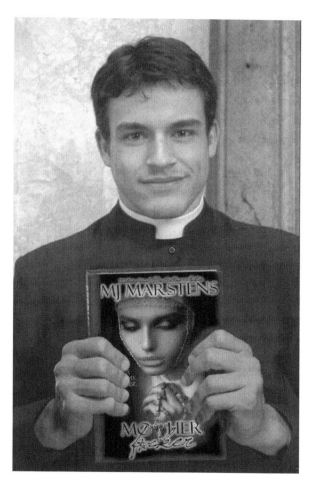

Father Hotness says, 'God Bless', and if you liked

this story, please consider leaving a review!

https://www.amazon.com/dp/B081DBKG6C

Long-winded Afterward

Soooooooooooo, as you all know, SEVEN DWARVES AND THE DAMNED APPLE was on pace to be released and fucking Motherfucker came and ruined it all. I'm so glad that it's out though. I love Evangeline like crazy. I might love her more than Zahra. DO NOT tell my other character that. She is super fucking crazy and I so don't want to deal with her shit.

So for those of you waiting patiently for my Snow White remake, thank you. It's hard to curb creativity. It's harder to curb craziness.

As usual, the world's BIGGEST thank you to my betas: Chan, Heather, Marlana, Lori, Rachael, and Regina. Not only do I appreciate that you read my craziness, but all the time and comments/corrections that you make for me. You guys are my first line of defense, and your unwavering support is like a hug to my heart. I love your faces in a way that borderlines disturbing.

A special thanks to my new PA, Kelly Grimes. This lady right here, W-O-W. Everyone else: be jealous;

because I seriously lucked out and got the world's greatest PA. No one pimps it like Kelly. I heart you, Kelly.

Of course, where would I be without my editor and formatter? I'll tell you: with a visually shitty-looking book that's also riddled with errors. So, THANK YOU to both Kathy Landis and Rozie Marshall for making my book shine.

THANK YOU to my ARC team! If you guys want to see an impressive collection of fun ladies, then check out my ARCers; because they are UH-MAY-ZING! I'm so very blessed to have each and every one of you reading and reviewing my work. Please note that I love your faces, too, in an equally disturbing manner.

A special shout out to Candace Diggs for posting about midget brothels in Gabrielle Ash's and Kat Blak's group; I think that might be my favorite part of this who fucked-up book, haha.

Another special shout out to Annie Lina. It was your post in RahRah that got this ball rolling. Thanks for the inspiration!

And, as always, thank you to YOU, my naughty, sinful reader. You know you're going to Hell for reading this, right? But I'll see you there. It's going to be one Hell of a party, ahahaha. (Bad pun, I know. Sorry. Sometimes I can't help myself; I think that I'm punny.)

I'm done now, I swear.

Coming Soon

Ephemeral (Liminal Academy 2) and **Eternal (Liminal Academy 3)** will be live surprise releases in 2019.

Seven Dwarves and the Damned Apple will be a surprise release in 2019.

Merry Elfin Christmas is a special RH comedic anthology that will be a live release on December 26th.

The Swan Empress (A Swan Lake retelling from my series **Classics Retold for RH**) coming December 29th. https://www.amazon.com/dp/B07ZPFYGQF

Scaled (A unique shifter retelling of Mulan from my series **Legends Retold for RH**) is coming this Chinese New Year, January 25th.

Mate Date (another comedic RH story with unique PNR and fated mates) coming Valentine's Day 2020. https://www.amazon.com/dp/B081SJS8HY

COMING IN MARCH 2020:

Looking for a BA lead lady who doesn't take any shit?

Then, you're in luck.

Sassafras (Sass for short) Dejais is coming your way with a whole lot of action and a whole lot of steam.

Keep an eye out for **Assassins of the Shadow Society (A.S.S)** series:

BADASS ALCHEMY (Book 1)

HARDASS ALCHEMY (Book 2)

KICKASS ALCHEMY (Book 3)

Also By MJ Marstens

VIRGO RISING

RETROGRADE

TOTAL LUNAR ECLIPSE

(The Afflicted Zodiac Series)

If you're looking for humor, craziness, steam, alpha assholes, and a very mouthy lead lady, then try this completed, unique series today. Available on KU.

EVANESCENT

(Liminal Academy I)

This spin-off academy series from The Afflicted Zodiac will have you in stitches as all your favorite characters return to tell Lilith's and Chiron's story.

331

UNVEILED: A DARK MÉNAGE

If you're looking for something dark, but deeply touching, then try this standalone. Available through Amazon and on KU, please read the trigger warning first.

ADVENTURES IN SUGARLAND

(Fairy Tales Retold for RH)

This naughty remake of Hansel and Gretel meets Candyland will have you craving sugar, and maybe something else. Full of all kinds of kinky fun, there are fetishes and taboo galore. Available through Amazon and on KU, please read the trigger warning first.

IMPRISMED

Captured in Rainbowland (Fairy Tales Retold for RH) In this colorful and hilarious romp, you get Alice in Wonderland mixed with a little Beauty in the Beast. Join

Wynn and her fucked up adventures in Rainbowland.

Available through Amazon and on KU.

Author Recommendations

Do you like the taboo found in this book? Maybe something dark and kinky like my books **UNVEILED** and **ADVENTURES in SUGARLAND**? Then try these authors:

Scarlett Snow

Tiegan Clyne

Loxley Savage

N.J. Adel

Maybe you're more into the laughs from a quirky lead lady like Mother Evangeline or Zahra and Lilith from my **AFFLICTED ZODIAC** series and **LIMINAL ACADEMY** series, then try:

Kat Quinn

Ann Denton

S.A. Parker

Jacquelyn Faye

Katie May

Raven Kennedy

Jaymin Eve/Jane Washington

Do you prefer something short, steamy, and hilarious liked **EXPOSED** from my **LASCIVIOUS LITTLES** series? Then try:

Madeline Fay

Maybe you need unique PNR and shifters like my upcoming books **THE SWAN EMPRESS** (Swan Lake retold), **SCALED** (Mulan retold), and **MATE DATE** (fated mates comedy), then try:

Jarica James

Laurel Skye

Regina J. Robinson

L.L. Frost

Laurel Chase

Serenity Rayne

Do you want amazing new worlds like in **IMPRSIMED: Captured in Rainbowland** and **ADVENTURES in SUGARLAND?** Then try:

Amy Sumida

Serena Lindahl

Avery Thorn

Maybe you need a *badass* lead lady, like Sassafras Dejais in my new series **ASSASSINS of the SHADOW SOCIETY (A.S.S.)**, then try something by:

Serena Nova

Winter Rose

A.J. Macey

Want to try some new authors? Then look no further than these amazing and upcoming stars:

Beth Rosalee (Fated wolf shifter book coming out Dec. 2nd)

Scarlett Ross (Contemporary office bully romance coming out Dec. 16th)

Gabrielle Ash and *Kat Blak (Occult/PNR coming out Feb. 1ˢᵗ.)*

Do you like big harems and you cannot lie? Maybe some m/m action? Then try *Rozie Marshall.*

Maybe you're feeling a little stabby? Then you need something by the one and only Murder Queen, *Bo Reid.*

Do you want some zombies and apocalyptic dystopia? Try *Maya Riley, Rowan Thalia, or Kristy Cunning.*

Need some YA/NA? Then definitely look into *R.M. Walker* and *H.A. Wills.*

Want the best place for fun and recommendations? Then head over to RahRah, or Reverse Harem Readers and Authors. You can't go wrong with this amazing group. The admins and members are beyond amazing. https://www.facebook.com/groups/ReverseHaremRA/

Want teasers and a whole lot of naughty fun? Then get your cute booty over to my group. I promise that you won't regret it. Mostly. Maybe. Just give it a try. Once you go naughty, that's how you'll party. https://www.facebook.com/groups/MJMarstensNR/

Want only one dick?

No.

The answer is no, but sometimes, there's a one-dick read that's so awesome you forget that you want all the dicks. Here are some of my favorite non-RH authors who make one-dick reading a one-click buy:

Laura Thalassa (PNR)

R.K. Lilley (contemporary BDSM)

Aleatha Romig (mindfuck books that blow your mind with their twists)

Amelia Hutchins (PNR)

Karen Marie Moning (PNR and damn if her series didn't have the hallmark of a good RH series in the making, too)

Qatarina Wanders (YA)

Made in the USA
Lexington, KY
07 December 2019